"Sorry, I didn't know you were out here."

"I didn't mean to be."

"I love sitting on the porch swing at night."

He scooted to the end, patted the slats beside him. "Feel free."

She hesitated a moment, but headed his way in the end.

"I don't know why I like it out here." She shuddered. "There're probably snakes lurking. Or bats. Or bears, for that matter. But I love the night sounds. You don't get that in the city."

"I imagine not."

"And the stars are so bright here. So many of them."

He scanned the horizon, ashamed he often took the stars for granted. "So why do you stay there?"

"It's where I belong. It's nice to visit the country but I could never live here. I'd be bored to tears."

With all his worries over his friends and her reminder that she was a city girl through and through, why did he feel so pulled toward Devree? Despite the warm night, a chill settled in deep. He had absolutely nothing in common with her. He better tread carefully.

Shannon Taylor Vannatter is a stay-at-home mom/pastor's wife/award-winning author. She lives in a rural central Arkansas community with a population of around one hundred, if you count a few cows. Contact her at shannonvannatter.com.

Books by Shannon Taylor Vannatter

Love Inspired

Texas Cowboys

Reuniting with the Cowboy
Winning Over the Cowboy
A Texas Holiday Reunion
Counting on the Cowboy

Love Inspired Heartsong Presents

Rodeo Ashes
Rodeo Regrets
Rodeo Queen
Rodeo Song
Rodeo Family
Rodeo Reunion

Counting on the Cowboy

Shannon Taylor Vannatter

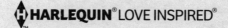
HARLEQUIN® LOVE INSPIRED®

Recycling programs for this product may not exist in your area.

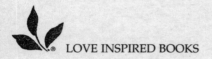

LOVE INSPIRED BOOKS

ISBN-13: 978-1-335-50942-0

Counting on the Cowboy

Copyright © 2018 by Shannon Taylor Vannatter

www.Harlequin.com

Printed in U.S.A.

And be ye kind one to another, tenderhearted,
forgiving one another, even as God
for Christ's sake hath forgiven you.
—*Ephesians* 4:32

To my parents.
I hate getting dirty, refuse to grow a vegetable garden and will never own farm animals, but I'm thankful y'all made a country girl out of me. Even though Logan says I'm too city.

Chapter One

Help! There's a goat on the roof!

Devree Malone typed the frantic text to her brother-in-law while edging the engaged couple she was showing around the ranch closer to the chapel.

If the goat would just keep quiet up there, maybe the soon-to-be newlyweds wouldn't notice and she wouldn't lose this gig. At least it was still April, as the cooler not-quite-seventy degree temperature meant the farm animal odors were at a minimum.

A dark truck turned into the drive and a cowboy climbed out: Stetson, Wranglers, boots. *Maybe a ranch hand?* His gaze went to the goat, then met hers as a smirk settled on his lips. One so charming she almost forgot about the goat.

Almost. *Do something, cute cowboy.* Hopefully, her mental plea would span the thirty or so feet between them. She guided the couple inside the chapel and tried to concentrate on the bride's excited chatter.

"Imagine burgundy roses on the lattice arbor with tulle trailing down the sides." If only she could have gone ahead and decorated. But the wedding was still two weeks away. "We'll put big poufy bows on the end of each pew."

For now, she needed to wow them with what she could. She flipped the switch, setting off a sea of twinkle lights woven among the exposed rafters above.

"Oh." The enchanted bride leaned her head against her groom's shoulder.

Why put so much into the wedding when the marriage would probably be history in less than a year? In her eight years of wedding planning, just under half her couples had divorced. And then there was the ceremony that got canceled when Devree discovered her boyfriend of six months was the groom-to-be.

Just stomach this last wedding.

A month in Bandera serving as the event planner at the Chasing Eden Dude Ranch would provide Devree the chance to help her brother-in-law. It would help make sure his very pregnant wife stayed on bed rest and brought Devree a healthy niece or nephew into the world.

If she nailed this nuptial, maybe the bride's wealthy father, Phillip Brighton would hire her to plan his Brighton Electronics company retreat. And she just might be able to leave her *I do* planning behind.

Something caught her eye out the window. The cowboy, feed bucket in hand, walking backward toward the barn. The goat clambered from the top of the pavilion, across the storage shed, onto the old storm shelter and then down to the ground.

Her gaze bounced back to the couple. Still enthralled with the twinkle lights.

"Instead of walking off to the side for the unity sand ceremony, what do you think about having a couple of groomsmen move it here in the middle of the aisle?"

Devree positioned herself where she thought it should go. "That way all you'd have to do is turn around."

It would be difficult enough to maneuver the bride's mile long train up and down the aisle once without adding the possibility of it getting tangled up in vases of sand.

"I love it." Miranda Brighton's eyes lit up. "That way I won't have to fight with my dress and our families and friends will be able to see better if we're up front and center." She pressed her face into her groom's shoulder. "I can't wait to be Mrs. Joel Anderson."

"I can't wait to be Mr. Joel Anderson."

The couple's giggles mingled, ending in a sweet kiss.

Devree looked away. She used to love weddings. Almost as much as the brides and grooms she'd worked with. Until Randall.

Just one more ceremony. If the goat didn't ruin it for her. Then, if she never got another glimpse of tulle and twinkle lights, she'd be a happy woman. And maybe, just maybe, this charming couple would make it.

"There are a few side rooms along the foyer connecting the fellowship hall in the back. Plenty of room for the wedding party to prepare for the ceremony."

"Thank you so much for meeting with us, Devree." Miranda never took her eyes off her groom-to-be. "I wanted Joel to see the chapel since he's only seen pictures online."

"I don't care where the ceremony takes place. The married part is all that matters to me." The requisite sappy response from Joel.

It would be nice if he kept feeling that way. But odds were—he wouldn't.

"Okay, I'll see you both for a consultation in a week." *Please let the goat be all lassoed and out of sight.* She led the way to the exit, praying as she went. Guilt stabbed. She shouldn't ask God for anything after ignoring Him for so long. Closing her eyes, she hesitated at the double doors, then swung them open and scanned the area. No goat. Her breath rushed out.

"Thank you." The giddy bride hugged her and the couple held hands as they strolled to their car.

"Excuse me." The cowboy behind her. "You work here?"

"Yes." She turned to face him. His Stetson shadowed pale green eyes, dark hair and a cleft chin. Enough to make a girl weak in the knees. Thankfully, she wasn't a girl anymore. She was a battle-scarred woman. "I'm the new wed—I mean—event planner." At least she hoped to leave nuptials behind. "Thanks for getting rid of the goat."

"I love goats." His gaze locked on hers, as if he had all day.

"Do you work here?"

"Not yet. Don't s'pose you'd know where I might find the owners? Do the Donovans still own this place?"

"My sister and her husband, Chase Donovan." She checked her phone. Chase hadn't responded to her frantic text.

"I used to be best buds with Chase."

"Really?"

"I lived here as a kid. You and your sister from around these parts?"

"No. We're from Aubrey. I live in Dallas, technically anyway. I'm just here for six weeks." Why was she telling him all this? Those magnetic eyes held her prisoner, kept her running at the mouth.

"What about Chase's little sister, Eden? She still around?"

"Um…she died three years ago."

"No." His shoulders drooped. "Not sweet little Eden."

His genuine sadness got under her skin. "A few years back. Scuba diving accident. She and my sister were

friends. That's how Landry and Chase ended up together."
She shoved her hands in her back pockets. "Speaking of
which, he's leading a trail ride, but Landry's inside. I'll
take you to her."

"I'd appreciate that."

She headed for the ranch house. His footfalls trailed
behind her.

Despite her sister's difficult pregnancy, the yard was
still a well-kept green oasis in the middle of yellowed
drought-ridden Texas Hill Country. Thanks to a nightly
dousing by sprinklers Chase had set up. She hugged herself, staying in the middle of the walkway, keeping as
much distance as possible from any lurking poison ivy or
rattlesnakes hiding in the suspicious-looking crape myrtle
bushes lining each side.

Would the cowboy disrupt Landry's calm? She stopped,
spun to face him.

He skidded to a stop.

"You're not going to stress her out, are you?"

The corner of his mouth hitched up. "Not planning on
it. Unless applying for a job does that to her."

"She usually doesn't hire the ranch hands. Chase does
that." She chewed on the inside of her cheek. "But he
should be back soon." She turned back toward the house.
But what had he done with the goat? She halted again and
swung around.

More space between them this time. He grinned, deep-
ening the cleft in his chin and awakening dimpled cheeks.
A dangerous combination. "Learned my lesson. Don't follow too close."

"Where is the goat?"

"Put him in that pen." He motioned to the rail fence
near the barn out back.

No goat in sight.

"Didn't think it would hold him long." He adjusted his hat. "Goats are notorious for getting out. Especially if they're alone. And I didn't see any others. Unless they all got out."

"I don't have a clue how many there are. I didn't know they had any until I saw the one on the roof. Thanks again for taking care of that. If my bride had seen him, she may have freaked out and changed venues."

"Count on me for goat wrangling." He searched the area. "If you find him again that is."

"I don't have any other appointments, so we'll let Chase worry about the goat." She strode toward the house again. Made it all the way this time.

As she stepped onto the porch, he passed her, opened the door and held it for her.

"Thanks." Why did her cheeks warm?

His boot heels clanked behind her as she led him through the lobby into the great room.

"Landry?"

"Oh, I'm so glad you're here." Landry lay on the couch, the mound of her seven-and-a-half-month pregnancy obvious. "I'm so bored. Tell me all about your meeting."

"We have company."

Landry craned her neck until the cowboy stepped into her line of vision.

"Sorry to bother you, ma'am."

"I'd get up, but my doctor insists I lay here like a bloated heifer."

"This is…" Devree faltered. She didn't even know the cowboy's name. What if he'd made that whole story up from stuff he'd found online? What if he was some robber or escaped convict? Why hadn't she thought of that? Constant guests at the dude ranch and the laid-back country lifestyle where everybody knew everybody had lessened her suspicious nature. Thankfully, Chase's chef dad was in the kitchen, only a scream away.

"Brock McBride. I'm here to apply for the handyman position."

"Oh, good. Please tell me you're qualified." Landry paused as she worked something on her phone. "I'm Landry Donovan, and this is my sister, Devree Malone."

"Nice meeting you, ma'am." He tipped his hat.

"My husband is leading a trail ride, but I just texted him and he should be back any minute."

"You might have a goat out." His gaze roamed the room, from the barn-wood ceiling and walls to the massive stone fireplace.

"Again?" Landry rolled her eyes.

"The crazy thing climbed up on the chapel roof. It's a wonder my jittery bride didn't see him, run screaming and cancel everything."

"I found the feed bucket and it went right in the pen." Brock took his hat off.

Landry grinned at Brock, then Devree. "Your hero."

Her skin heated to boiling. "I said thank you." She shot her sister a look. "But I'm not in the market for a hero."

"Good. Because the goat was out again by the time they left." His mouth twitched. "Besides, my cape's at the dry cleaner, and in my experience, damsels are more trouble than they're worth."

"How's my princess?" Chase entered the great room, his focus solely on Landry. Worry evident in his furrowed brow. "Are you following orders?"

"I've been here all day, I promise. And baby Donovan is kicking up a storm." Landry motioned to Brock, introduced him and explained why he was here.

Chase's frown relaxed and a wide grin took over. "Brock McBride?"

"The one and only."

The two men hugged with lots of back clapping.

So he'd told the truth about knowing Devree's brother-in-law.

"Guess y'all know each other." Landry rolled onto her side.

"Brock used to live here. We grew up together. He's Becca's son."

Landry's eyes widened.

"Becca, the housekeeper?" Devree turned to Brock. But her last name wasn't McBride.

His face went ashen.

"She'll be so excited to see you." Landry's mouth curved into a smile. "Does she know you're here?"

"Uh—maybe I should come back some other time." Brock took a step back.

"No. Timing's perfect." Chase slapped him on the back again. "Let's go to the office. Unless you want to let your mom know you're here first."

"No," he replied, a hint of dread in his tone. He cleared his throat. "I should have called first. And I have another appointment. I'll have to get back to you."

"But you can't leave without seeing your mom." Chase steered him to the foyer. "She's just upstairs cleaning the guest rooms."

Seconds later, the great room door closed.

"What was that all about?" Devree sank into the chair facing her sister.

"I didn't make the connection when he first introduced himself, but Becca mentioned she was married before Ron and worked here back when Chase was a kid. Chase told me he and Brock were friends until Brock's dad died when he was young and Becca moved away." Landry scrolled down her phone, tapped and pressed it to her ear. "Becca came back several years ago, but she and Brock have been estranged. She's longed to reconnect with him for years. And now, he's here. She'll be so excited."

"Maybe we shouldn't get involved in their private business. Besides, I think he's leaving."

"He's probably nerv—Becca. You won't believe who's here. Brock," her sister said, ignoring Devree's words of caution. "Yes, I'm sure. Chase is in the foyer talking to him as we speak."

An audible squeal came through the phone.

"Hurry, Devree," Landry begged. "You have to stop him. If he leaves before Becca can get to him, it'll break her heart."

Surely, he wouldn't leave without seeing Becca. Always so sweet and pleasant—who could be estranged from her?

She should stay out of it. But if she did, she knew Landry would try to stop Brock from leaving. And her sister didn't need any more stress. On top of that, the ranch badly needed a handyman.

Devree dashed toward the foyer.

"Please don't leave without seeing your mom." Chase stepped in front of the exit, cutting off Brock's escape.

"It's been a while. I should have called first," Brock repeated through gritted teeth.

"Look, I don't know what happened between y'all. All I know is your mom has pined for you—the entire fifteen years since she came back here."

Fifteen years. His mom had been at the dude ranch for that long. Miss City Girl—who'd nagged Dad to move—had come back willingly and stayed? Probably the only place she could find a job, considering her habit. But if his mom was still using, would Chase keep her on? Surely not. Unless she somehow hid her addiction.

Footfalls behind him; he braced himself.

"Wait!" The wedding planner.

He'd enjoyed talking to her, despite their being from different worlds. Until Chase mentioned his mom.

"Landry called Becca. She's on her way. You can't just leave."

"I'll leave when I'm good and ready." He spun to face her. "And I'm good and ready."

She gasped at his outburst and something flashed in her eyes. Hurt.

"I'm sorry." He hung his head. "I didn't mean to snap at you. It's just—there's history to wade through. And I didn't bring my muck boots." He turned and strode for the door, intent on going through Chase if he had to.

"Brock!" The voice he dreamt about too often for peace of mind echoed down the staircase behind him and took him back in time. Ten years old, sobbing on the social worker's shoulder, wondering when his mom would come back for him.

Never.

For the last fifteen years, she'd been here. And never lifted a finger to try to find him.

The sound of hurried footsteps descended on his ears. Pressure built in his chest. He didn't turn around.

"Please wait!" A small hand grabbed his arm. "Please." Pleading, tearful. "At least look at me."

She stepped in front of him. Much the way he remembered her. Rail thin, long brown hair. Eighteen years older. But somehow she looked better. Healthier. No telltale sunken shadows beneath her pale blue eyes. The hand on his arm was steady.

"Sure hope you'll stick around, Brock." Chase gave him a beseeching smile. "The job's yours."

"You didn't even look at my résumé." He focused on his friend, mainly to escape his mom's imploring gaze.

Why did he still think of her as his mom after she'd abandoned him?

"I'm familiar with your work and you're overqualified. Your mom found an article about you building luxury cabins in a magazine a few years back."

"I still have it." She squeezed his arm.

Why did she think she had the right to touch him? He pulled away from her grasp, took a step back.

Her hand fell to her side. "Please stay."

"We'll give you some privacy." Chase stepped away from the exit, motioned Devree to follow.

"I need to stash my wedding paraphernalia in the chapel loft." A pinched frown drew her brows together. Her gaze clashed with his, and then she whirled away and disappeared outside. Was she embarrassed to witness their turmoil? Did she feel sorry for him? Or for his mom?

"Please, Brock, can't we talk? You came here for a reason. Don't back out now."

His mom's plea clanged in his head. He'd come for the job. But also because the eight years he'd spent at the dude ranch were the best of his life. When his dad had been alive. When his mom hadn't been catatonic and actually cared if he ate or not. Before their move to Dallas. Before they lost their apartment and ended up moving in with his alcoholic grandfather. Before she got hooked on drugs.

He'd returned to come to terms with his past and his mom's abandonment. To remember his dad. He'd expected to come face to face with the memories that haunted him. But not with her.

"Please come to the office with me." Tears streamed down her cheeks.

But not as many as he'd cried over her. "I didn't know you were here."

"Or you wouldn't have come." She hiccuped a sob. "I get that. Can't we just talk for a few minutes?"

"Do the Donovans know everything? I mean, about you."

She sucked in a big breath, shook her head. "Granny did, but she's been gone several years. I told everyone else your father's family turned you against me and we haven't spoken in years."

"So you expect me to stay and live your lie with you?" He glanced at the door, seeking escape. "I don't think so. Tell Chase bye for me."

"But you can't leave." She blocked him off, set her hand on his arm again.

"I'm leaving now. Please get out of my way. I think I've had enough of memory lane."

"I wish you'd stay. Jesus forgave me. For everything. Can't you give me a chance?"

How dare she pull the Jesus card.

"If you stay, I'll give you space. And if you give me some time, I'll summon up the courage to tell the truth."

"I'll think about it." If it would get her out of his way, he'd think about all she'd said. All the way to his truck. All the way back to Waco.

She stepped aside.

He practically bolted out the door, down the porch steps and across the pristine yard to the parking lot.

But Devree, with the sun setting her cinnamon hair aflame, waited by his truck. Blocking his escape.

"Could you tell Chase I'll call him?" He willed her to step aside.

Her brilliant blue gaze locked on his. "Please don't go."

A heartfelt plea from a beautiful woman. Normally he couldn't resist that. Even though it was obvious the redhead was just the type he needed to steer clear of: a city girl.

Just like his mom. And he certainly didn't want anything to do with her. He needed to get out of Dodge. Fast.

Chapter Two

Devree's face heated when she realized he could have taken her plea for him to stay as her own. "I mean, Chase could use you around here."

"I'm sure he can find someone else." Brock shifted his weight, obviously wanting her to move out of his way.

But she had to convince him to stay. For her sister's sake. And Becca's too. "The chapel's completed, but they're still in the middle of expanding the ranch. Their new house, along with honeymoon and hunting cabins are in progress. Chase is up to his eyeballs with all of it and the handyman bailed."

"Surely there've been other applicants."

"Several who would be great as ranch hands, but painfully inexperienced when it comes to fixing anything other than fences." She drew in a long breath.

"I can't stay here."

"I have a wedding scheduled next month. Plus, they've got more weddings starting in June and wild boar hunts booked through fall with guests expecting cabins ready for their stay. Meanwhile, there are a dozen projects that need attention and a very pregnant lady who'd like to be in her new house before the baby comes. Please say you'll take the job."

"I can't do this. Not with—"

"Landry had a stillbirth last spring." Her vision blurred at the memory of the tiny casket.

His shoulders sagged. "I'm sorry. Chase didn't say anything."

"They don't like to dwell on it. It's too hard." She blinked the moisture away. "She's almost lost this baby twice and is still having complications. She can't handle any more stress. Chase needs to spend more time keeping her calm. Just stay until Chase can find someone else. My niece or nephew's life could depend on it."

His eyes softened. "No pressure."

"Sorry." Devree kicked at the gravel drive. "They're scared to death. And so am I." She managed to get a hold on her emotions, looked back up at him. "Here's your chance to help an old friend. With a baby's life hanging in the balance."

"You drive a hard bargain." He looked skyward. "I'll stay on one condition."

"Which is?"

"I don't want to talk about my mother. And I don't want any of you pushing me toward her."

"We owe you." She offered her hand. His rough, calloused palm dwarfed hers.

"And only until Chase can hire someone else."

"Come on. Let's go tell them." She jogged to the ranch house.

With his long stride, he stayed right with her even though he was only walking. He beat her to the porch, climbed the steps and opened the door for her.

"Do you think your mom is okay?"

His gaze went steely. "Don't know."

And obviously didn't care.

"And that counts as talking about her."

"I can't help it if I'm worried about her." In the last year since the dude ranch started hosting weddings, Devree had planned a handful here. Becca helped decorate and clean after each one—a real sweetheart. How could he not care about her?

"You're still talking about her."

"Sorry." She stepped inside, hurried across the foyer to the great room.

Landry was right where she'd left her—laying on the couch, feet in her husband's lap.

"Good news. Brock agreed to take the job."

"Wonderful." Landry's relief whooshed out in a heavy sigh.

"Glad to hear it." Chase's smile went a mile wide.

"Where should I bunk?"

"Go out to the barn, ask for Troy. He'll get you settled in a room at the bunkhouse where a lot of the hands stay."

"Sounds like a plan. I'd like to tackle the goat problem. Exactly how many are missing?"

"Eleven. Six does—one is gestating with a kid due in the next few weeks—and five bucks. All pygmies. We're planning a petting zoo by the time school's out."

Does and bucks? Weren't those deer? Gestating with a kid due? Did that translate into pregnant goat? Devree was desperately behind on her ranch and farm animal lingo.

"They need something to occupy them so they'll stay in the pens."

Apparently, Brock knew a thing or two about goats. Or does and bucks and kids. Or whatever they were.

"Use whatever you need out of the lumber pile in the barn." Chase adjusted the comforter around Landry's feet. "I'd also appreciate it if you'd arrange for demolition of that old storm shelter on the east side of the chapel. It's an eyesore and goat magnet. Besides, we have a basement so we don't need it."

"Sure. First thing in the morning."

"And, Devree, since we have a handyman now, I need to add to your load."

"Okay?" *Hopefully, nothing dirty or stinky.*

"Our event schedule is kind of dead between spring break and June. Which will leave you at loose ends. With Landry down for the count, our last handyman's wife was supposed to handle decorating the chapel and the honeymoon cottages. I was wondering if you could help with that."

"Um, I'm a wed—event planner. Not an interior decorator." Especially not a rustic one. Country-themed weddings were always a challenge for her.

"Please don't let Chase do it." Landry groaned. "Everything will end up looking just like the hunting cabins. With dead wild boar heads on the walls."

And cause her sister stress. "I guess I could try."

"You'll do great." Landry sounded so certain. "With all your experience at decorating venues for weddings. For the chapel, just a few decor items. Keep it simple and rustic with a few crosses and burlap. And for the cabins, pick some paint colors, tile and flooring. We get all our decor items, furnishings, drapery and bedding from Resa's store. She'll give you good advice."

"I'm on it."

"Great." Chase relaxed, ran his fingers along the bottom of Landry's toes, eliciting a giggle out of her. "I'll need you and Brock to focus on the chapel and Gramp's fishing cabin to begin with."

"Why the fishing cabin?" Devree tried not to cringe.

She'd much rather work in one of the new structures instead of an old abandoned one.

"With a wedding in two weeks and the new cabins unfinished—" Landry adjusted her pillow "—it'll be quicker to transform the fishing cabin into a honeymoon hideaway than finishing one of the others."

"But no one's lived in the cabin since I moved out after our wedding. Becca cleaned it—" Chase winced as he obviously realized he'd brought up a sore subject "—but it needs caulk around the plumbing and trim work."

Right on cue, the muscle in Brock's jaw had flexed at the mention of his mother. "I'll check it out and tackle it in the morning." His words came out clipped, his mind still obviously on whatever his issues were with Becca.

"It should be vacant by now." Landry cringed. "Chase set mouse traps."

That bit of info almost stopped Devree's heart. She squelched a shudder. Surely, there wouldn't be any critters. Not live ones, anyway.

"I'll try to find where they're getting in," Brock promised.

"We'll be fine," she assured her sister and Chase. But would *she*? With mice? If there were rodents, there might be snakes or worse…spiders. "Don't worry about a thing. Y'all just concentrate on baby Sprint."

"Sprint?" Landry squinted one eye, her thinking mode.

"I figure his or her dad is Chase, so she or he is Sprint."

Landry's giggle mixed with Chase's chuckle. A nice relaxed sound. Just what she wanted to hear from her sister.

She turned to see that she'd even elicited a grin out of Brock.

"No matter what y'all name the baby, that's what I'm

calling him or her." She shot her sister a wink. "I've still got boxes of wedding decorations to stash in the chapel."

"You'll need help." Landry smoothed her hands over the roundness of her belly.

"I'm on it." Chase moved Landry's feet, started to get up.

"Stay put," Brock ordered. "I'll help her."

"That's not in your job description."

"She's your top priority." Brock pointed at Landry. "I'm here. Let me help."

Chase settled Landry's feet back in his lap. "I appreciate that."

So, Brock could be caring—just not toward his mother. Despite the tension, it would be nice to have someone else take part of Chase's load so he could focus on Landry. And given time, maybe Becca and Brock could work things out.

He followed her to her car where they each grabbed a stack of plastic containers and headed for the chapel.

She hadn't anticipated working with the broad-shouldered, way too good-looking cowboy. But she couldn't let him distract her.

Without shifting his load, he shouldered the door to the chapel open and held it for her. "Where do you want these?"

"On the back pew will be fine."

He set down her containers. "Is that all?"

"Yes." It would help if he stashed everything in the loft for her, but that would mean having him stick around. "Thanks. I can take it from here."

He tipped his hat and exited. Through the side window, she saw him hurry toward the long building that housed a dozen hands and the foreman, Troy. His temporary home.

She had to concentrate on the chapel and the fishing cabin. Not the cowboy.

* * *

Barely daylight, Brock nailed the final board into place on the play station in the goat pen. A buck, barely two feet tall, nibbled his elbow. And they said cats were curious.

"Just give me a minute, little guy, and I'll get out of your way." He gathered his tools, slipped them in his belt and took a step back. Just as soon as he was out of the way, all five bucks climbed on the station, wrestling their way to the top. The matching structure in the doe's pen was getting used as well. He slipped out the gate, fastened it back.

He'd never built such a thing, but he'd gotten ideas off the internet last night. Apparently, good ones. With wire fencing in place and two more wooden rails at the top, they should stay in now.

Next on the agenda, he planned to caulk the fishing cabin and make the repairs there. He needed to keep busy. Keep his mind off the pretty redhead. And his mother. On his first official day as handyman, he'd already set up a time for the demolition of the old storm cellar by the chapel.

He loaded an assortment of lumber he hadn't used into his truck and drove over to the barn. Once the fishing cabin and Chase's new house were complete, getting his friend moved before the baby came would be his priority.

After that, he'd focus on whatever else needed fixing. But hopefully, he wouldn't be here long.

As he stacked the wood neatly back where he'd found it, a prickle of awareness swept over him. Someone watching. He glanced around and saw movement in the loft. A moment later, a child's head popped up, then ducked again.

"Are you supposed to be up there alone?"

Busted, she came out of hiding, peered down at him. "My grandpa had to take guests to their room and I sort of slipped out. But I'm real careful when I climb in the loft and I can hear the bus when it gets to Cheyenne's house. She lives next door. Once I hear it, I can run to the road. And I'm real fast." She climbed down to reveal light brown hair and freckles. First grade maybe.

"You shouldn't slip out on your grandpa like that. He'll worry."

"I'll be back before he knows I'm gone. I'm Ruby."

"I'm Brock."

"I know who you are." She plopped on a hay bale. "You're my uncle."

A hollow weight settled in his chest. Had his mom had another child—his sibling?

"But I'm not supposed to tell anybody. It's me and Mama's secret. I'm real good at keeping secrets. I figured you already knew, so I don't gotta keep it from you."

He swallowed hard. "So who's your mama?"

"You haven't met her yet. Her name's Scarlet. My grandma's favorite color was red. So she named Mama Scarlet and Mama named me Ruby to memorialize her."

"Like I said, you best get back before your grandpa misses you."

She gasped. "There's the bus." She waved, then bolted for the ranch house as fast as her little legs would carry her. Minutes later, he heard the bus stop at the end of the drive. It didn't tarry long before driving past.

Scarlet? Did he have a sister? But red had never been his mom's favorite color. At least when he'd lived with her anyway. Maybe the child was confused? Or playing a game?

A scream echoed through the morning stillness.

Brock bolted in the direction it came from.

Another shriek from Gramp's old fishing cabin.

He charged full force.

On the porch, Devree held something small with pliers.

She dropped both with a screech and did a little dance in her high heels.

"What's wrong?"

She whirled in his direction, her business-style skirt slim-fitting at her knees. Wild-eyed, mouth open and pulled down at the corners, she looked ready to let out another blood-curdling shriek. She sucked in a breath, shuddered. "A mouse. Its tail was caught in a trap."

"Where?" He climbed the porch steps, tried to hold in his laughter.

She propped her hands on her hips. "It's not funny. I turned it loose." She pointed to the end of the cabin. "It ran off over there."

He took in the trap laying nearby along with two sets of pliers. "You know," he said, unable to control his grin. "If you turn it loose, it'll most likely come right back in."

"I couldn't take all that squealing." She covered her ears with both hands. "From the moment I got here. Snap! Snap! Snap! And the poor little thing went to squealing."

"What's wrong?" Chase sprinted in their direction still wearing his robe.

"Nothing." Her hands dropped away from her head. "I didn't wake Landry did I?"

"No." His brows rose. "Why were you screaming about nothing?"

She repeated her story, shrugged as if it was no big deal. "When I turned him loose, he darted toward my foot. I might have yelled a bit. Just a little adrenaline kicking in. But I'm fine. And the mouse is too."

"You should have killed him." Chase tightened the belt on his robe. "He'll only come back inside."

"I know, but he was crying. And he was kind of cute."

Chase cut his gaze to the sky, as if trying to keep from rolling his eyes. "Are there any dead ones in other traps?"

She pulled in a shaky breath. "I think so."

"I'll empty them for you."

"I'll take care of it." Brock stepped up on the porch. "Just tell me where they are."

"Under the kitchen and bathroom counters, behind the trash can in the kitchen, living room and bedroom."

"I'm on it. What about getting some cats?"

"Good idea." Chase ran a hand through his bed head. "If you have any more live ones, call me."

"I'm fine." She pulled on a brave smile.

"And try not to scream. It scares the guests." Chase strolled back toward the ranch house.

Poor guy—completely stressed out.

"Let's just say I'm not the most serene person when it comes to rodents."

"I noticed." Brock smirked. "Guess you won't be helping me with the traps."

She shot him a look, then hung her head. "I think I'll hide in the closet while you take care of things. Landry can do anything—help birth farm animals, decapitate a rattlesnake with a hoe, bait her own fishing hook. But I'm not like that. Not at all."

A definite understatement from what little he knew of her so far.

"Sounds like it'll be a challenge to keep Landry occupied for six weeks." He peered down at her. "You really here for events? Or to help Chase babysit her without her knowing it?"

"Chase called, wanted me to help out here. They happened to have the first wedding booked in the new chapel." She shrugged. "It worked out perfectly."

"Kind of sounds like you were meant to be here." He hooked his thumbs through his belt loops.

"Except that I'm trying to go in a new direction as an

event planner—company retreats, family reunions, conferences, corporate Christmas parties—that sort of thing. But my sister needed me, so I'm doing this *one last wedding*." Bitterness edged her words. "And that's it." She stepped inside.

Her distaste for nuptials didn't detract from her beauty. Not at all.

He followed. Several large white-tailed and axis deer preserved in taxidermy mounts hung on the wall. A large glass display box full of fish hooks of every size and style, from hand-tied fly to vintage wooden lures. It had always fascinated him as a kid when he'd come here with Chase and Gramps.

"This place creeps me out." Devree shivered, hugged herself tighter.

"I always loved it. Gramps—he insisted everyone call him that—used to bring us here for early morning fishing." The smell of Pine Sol and lemon cleaning supplies tickled his nose. Took him back.

Since he always wanted to help when he made the cleaning rounds with his mom, she'd let him dust the guest rooms. He could almost feel the damp, worn terry cloth in his hand. The way he got two nightstands and a headboard dusted in the time it took her to clean an entire room and bathroom. But she'd never hurried him or reprimanded him for taking too long.

He shook the memories away. But his brush with Ruby settled in his empty spaces. "Do you know a little girl named Ruby?"

"Sure. She's Ron's granddaughter. She comes here to catch the bus some mornings and gets off here in the afternoon part of the time."

"I met her in the barn this morning. And Ron is?"

"Your um—Becca's husband. He's a bellhop and wild boar hunting guide here at the dude ranch."

So Mom had remarried. The muscle in his jaw twitched. "And Scarlet?"

"Ron's daughter."

His stepsister. It all clicked into place. Well, Ruby was cute and all, but he had no intention of getting to know his blended family while he was here.

"They're really sweet people." Devree settled on the plaid couch. "I need to get a feel for the space." She must have sensed he didn't want to talk about it. She tucked her feet up beside her. Probably trying to avoid varmints.

He scanned the room. With the blinds open, sunlight streamed into the main living area. There were wood floors, ceilings and log walls with a dozen marble eyes staring at them.

"It's perfect as is for a hunting cabin. Why not take the personal items out, spruce it up a bit and use it for that?"

"We need a honeymoon cottage up and running ASAP. And the guest cottages are all on the front of the property while the hunting ones are on the back of the acreage."

"But this is such a personal space. Why are they opening it up to guests?"

"Chase doesn't want it to go unused and eventually rot away. A ranch hand is coming sometime to take all these poor dead animals to the new house. Along with those." She gestured to the fishhook display with another shudder.

Snap! Another trap went off and she jumped. "Great. Another victim. Isn't there any other way?"

"I could buy some poison. But you take the chance of one dying in the wall. Trust me, you don't want to go there."

"Ugh." She closed her eyes. "Something humane?"

"There are live traps that don't hurt them. I'm going into town later to buy lumber. I could pick up a few."

"Say you do that and we catch them. Then what do we do to keep them from coming back in?"

"I could feed them to my pet boa constrictor."

Her eyes popped open wide, revealing a hint of green amidst the blue.

Captivating. "Kidding. I'd find some place deep in the woods."

"But what would they eat?"

"Seeds, berries. Don't worry, I'll find a good place for them."

"I'd appreciate it."

He went in the kitchen, came back with two traps.

She clasped a hand over her mouth.

"Sorry. You might not want to watch." He hurried to the door, emptied the traps several yards from the cabin and returned.

She buried her face in a pillow, stayed huddled on the couch while he made another trip with the remaining traps. Finished, he returned to the kitchen and washed his hands.

"You don't want me to reset them?"

"Definitely not." She peeked from behind the pillow.

"Okay, I'll bring the live traps by later. Anything else I can do for you before I start caulking?"

Her gaze darted to the glass display case hanging on the wall. "Could you do something with that?"

"The fishhooks?"

"Yes, please. If you laugh, I'll die, but I'm terrified of them."

Seriously? But the terror in her eyes kept his humor at bay. He opened the case.

"No!" She screeched. "Just take the whole thing." She closed her eyes. "I mean, it would be awful if you lost one."

"Or if one fell out."

"Stop." She pressed her face in the pillow again. "You'll give me nightmares."

"Relax. I was only checking to see how it's mounted. Have you been hooked?"

She lowered the pillow. With a slow nod, she rubbed the skin between her thumb and forefinger on her right hand, a slight scar. "My father promised to take Landry and me fishing when we were little. But someone called in sick and he had to work in the Christian bookstore our parents own. I got a hook out and tried to put it on my line so we'd be ready when he got home."

"And hooked yourself."

She pinched the skin. "It went through right here. All the way through, barb and all. It had to be cut out in the emergency room. I can still feel it."

Her vulnerability tugged at him as he shut the display case, carefully lifted the brackets off the screws holding it up. "I'll take it to the new house when I finish insulating. For now, how about I put it out of sight, maybe under the bed?"

"Thanks."

"So, do you like to fish?"

Her laugh came out ironic. "No. I'm afraid of hooks, worms are slimy and fish are stinky. I just wanted to be with my dad."

"Did you not get much time with him?"

"He was great at setting up outings with us. But we'd have these awesome plans until someone called in sick and he'd end up at the store. Sometimes, I went to work with him, just to be with him."

She was way too charming when she showed this soft side. "My dad died when I was barely eight."

"I bet that was tough." Her gaze met his.

"It was. He was my hero." The loss burned fresh in his

heart. He tucked the display case under his arm and headed for the bedroom.

"Thanks."

"Let me know if you need anything else."

"Thought your cape was at the dry cleaners. And I'll remind you, that despite circumstances, I'm not a damsel." A small smile slipped out. "Just slightly out of my element."

"Got my cape back this morning and we're in dire straits here. Mice and traps and fishhooks! Oh, my!" He mimicked the classic *Wizard of Oz* chant and got a chuckle out of her. And coming to her rescue might have its perks. She certainly wasn't a chore to look at.

"Just for the record, I'm afraid of flying monkeys too."

"Let me know if you see any of those." He shot her a wink and stashed the display box under the bed. "Typical city girl."

"I may be a city girl." Her tone turned sharp. "But there's nothing typical about me."

Definitely overly sensitive. And now he'd offended her. Maybe that was a good turn of events. The last thing he needed was to develop a soft spot for her.

Besides, he wouldn't be here long. And she wouldn't either. They were just biding their time stuck here together. Both itching to get back to their real lives.

Chapter Three

Devree drove past the ranch house and pulled into the cabin parking lot. Maybe she could do this. Once the ranch hands had removed all the dead animal heads yesterday, ideas for the cabin's decor took shape. A mix of rustic and shabby chic. This morning, her visit to Rustick's Log Furnishings had been productive.

Resa—store owner, neighbor and friend—had been extremely helpful. And, so Landry wouldn't feel useless, Devree had texted her pictures of her choices. With her sister's approval, she'd purchased a back seat full of curtains, pillows and a bedspread while the furniture would arrive next week.

Arms laden with goodies, she stepped up on the porch and reached blindly to insert the key into the lock. But the door opened.

Brock. "Here, let me help you." He tugged the bags out of her hands.

"Thanks." Why did his accidental touch send a shiver through her? Even after he'd called her *typical* just yesterday.

"You've been busy. Me too. I caulked all the plumbing

and popped all the trim to seal the joints. Where do you want this stuff?"

"On the couch. New furniture will arrive next week. Will it be in your way?"

"I should be done with the messy stuff by then." He stashed the bags, then grabbed a putty knife, scraped a spot on the log wall and wiped the area with a cloth. "What about the old furniture?"

"Chase is sending ranch hands. Most of it will go in his man cave at the new house. What doesn't will go to charities. Will you be doing any work in the bedroom or bathroom? I thought I'd put curtains up in there."

"Go for it. Need a screwdriver?"

Why did he have to be so helpful? And appealing? "Come to think of it…"

"Have you ever hung curtains?"

"Hello? I have my own apartment."

"Just offering my help. And a step stool."

"That might be useful."

He picked up a small stool from the corner, dug around in his toolbox. "Flat or Phillips?"

"Phillips."

"You know your way around a screwdriver." He handed it to her.

"I have a dad, you know." When she saw his gaze drop, she wished she could take that back. She hadn't meant to hurt him; it had just slipped out. "Thanks." She grabbed the bag, hoofed it to the bedroom.

Brock followed, carrying the stool. "Sure you don't need any help?"

"I've got this." She turned to take the stool from him. Something scampered across her sandaled foot. She screamed, dropped the screwdriver and the stool.

"What?"

But she was too busy clambering onto the bed. Safely off the floor, she stood in the middle, scanning for movement.

"What?" His tone exasperated.

"I think—" she did a whole body shudder followed by a heebie-jeebies dance "—a mouse just ran across my foot."

"Okay." He reached for her hand. "Just calm down. Sit and relax before you fall off there and break your neck."

"I'd really like to get out of here." She gingerly sat down in the center of the bed, keeping her eyes on the edges, half expecting a mouse to come climbing up the bed skirt.

"Maybe that's best." He gestured toward the door.

"I'm afraid to put my feet on the floor." She squeezed her eyes closed. Great. She'd just proven every city girl notion he had about her to be true.

"Do I need to carry you?"

Her eyes popped open, surveyed him for a moment. Feet on the floor with the mice? Or carried out by the handsome cowboy she barely knew? Which was worse? Definitely rodents. With a slow nod, she scooted toward him.

He scooped her up.

With no choice, she put her arms around his neck, tried not to cling too tight.

As he stepped out on the porch, an elderly couple hand in hand rounded the walking trail thirty feet away.

"Look, Henry, newlyweds."

"In my day, you carried her inside, young man." The man frowned. "Not out."

"Thanks for the advice."

As her cheeks flamed, she felt the deep rumble of Brock's laughter. "You can put me down now."

He bent to lower her. "You know it was probably the same mouse you let go yesterday."

"Not funny." She smacked him on the shoulder.

imal smells. And goats are kind of fun. It's like they're playing king of the mountain. I want to see who wins."

"Knock yourself out." He tipped his hat, continued on to the cabin. Typical, but with a few surprises.

"I'll be there once you get it all evacuated."

He hurried down the path, eager to escape the scent of her apple shampoo. A scent that he was starting to recognize as uniquely hers. Just one more reason Chase needed to find another handyman and Brock needed to go on down the road.

As he stepped up onto the porch of the fishing cabin, a thud sounded at the back. Not Devree. Maybe the ranch hands were moving the old furniture out today.

He turned the knob, but it was still locked. He inserted the key, clicked the latch, opened the door. Just inside, a tightly woven wire cage with the grid open, a dozen mice still inside. "Huh?"

It was a live trap for larger animals, not the kind he'd bought. And besides, he'd put his traps in the bedroom and kitchen. He shut the wire grid, keeping the rodents locked inside, hurried toward the kitchen.

The window in the top of the live trap he'd set revealed it was empty, the release open. The back door stood ajar. He hurried out, looked around. Caught a glimpse of a man wearing a baseball cap a hundred yards away.

"Hey! What are you doing?"

The man bolted for the woods.

Brock shot after him, down the trail, past the barn and into the pine thicket behind it.

The runner stayed off the trail. Briars clawed at Brock's jeans. Some jabbed into tender flesh. The trees and undergrowth were so dense he couldn't see the guy anymore, just followed the sound of his escape. Prayed he didn't blindly step on a rattler.

A branch swatted him in the face. Eyes tearing up, he couldn't see a thing. Still, he was caught off guard when he stepped in a hole, his knee buckling, and he went down. He jumped up quick, but it was quiet as he peered into the dense sea of green. Nothing, as he stood there and listened for several minutes.

Why would the man put mice in the cabin? He headed back toward the structure. It explained the constant infestation. And brought up a whole host of new questions.

Devree kept her eyes on the ground. Aware that snakes slithered in the cool of the morning and evening this time of year, she stayed on the path to the fishing cabin.

The rooster crowed again, close by. Surely, the guests hated him as much as she did.

"I'm up already," she growled. "Can't you just sleep in sometimes?"

A flash of red to her left. The rooster running at her.

She bolted for the fishing cabin, snakes forgotten, but the rooster cut her off. A flap of amber-colored wings, blue-and-green tail feathers, spurs aimed at her as he lunged/flew in her direction. She dodged, bit her tongue to keep from screaming. No waking Chase again or alerting Brock to come to her rescue. She scrambled around Rusty. He crowed in hot pursuit. Okay, maybe she wouldn't mind if Brock showed up about now.

"You stupid bird, leave me alone." She made it to the cabin porch, grabbed a broom, spun and jabbed it at the rooster.

He paced back and forth, looking cocky, crowed again, then turned and headed up the path back to the barn.

"Take that, you stupid rooster." But as much as she wanted to, she couldn't just leave him loose to attack guests. She followed at a distance. Not a ranch hand in sight to help her.

Instead of going to his coop, the rooster stopped near the goat pen, pecked at the ground. Though she'd never been inside the barn, if she could find some feed, maybe she could lure the foul fowl back into his lair.

At least he was the only one out. She rounded the goat pen, found a bucket near the chicken coop with seeds in it, opened the wire door of the pen, and jogged back to the huge bird. But not too close.

"Look what I got, big fella."

The rooster cocked his head, strutted in her direction. Faster than she was comfortable with, but she still had the broom. She backed all the way to the pen, then threw the bucket inside. Thankfully, the rooster went in and she fastened the door in place.

She blew out a big breath, closed her eyes, leaned her forehead on the hand that was still holding the broom.

A noise behind her. She jabbed the broom as she spun around.

And almost gouged Brock in the chest.

His arms went up in a defensive stance. "I never would have pegged you for having such impressive rooster wrangling skills."

She dropped the broom, covered her face with her hands. "Sorry. I thought Rusty had a friend."

"I doubt he has any with that attitude. Whoa! Get back in there." Brock scooped up the broom, darted around her. "No wonder he got out, there's a hole in the pen."

By the time she turned around, Brock had the broom clamped over the hole. The rooster flapped his wings and crowed, but at least he wasn't going anywhere.

"That's weird." Brock knelt, inspected the wire.

"What?"

"It's been cut. With wire cutters." He ran his fingers along the slit. "See how it's crimped—dull wire cutters do that."

"Why would someone cut the wire?"

"I have no idea. But probably for the same reason they'd bring a live trap full of mice to the cabin."

"Huh?" She shuddered. "Someone opened the trap you set?"

He told her about the extra trap and chasing the man he'd dubbed Ball-Cap into the woods.

"He broke in?" Her voice cracked. "Do you know who he was?"

"I couldn't get a good look. He was too far away. But I don't know many folks around here, anyway."

"So someone's been bringing mice to the fishing cabin. And they cut the wire, so the rooster would get out. Why would anyone do that?"

"I'm not sure. But once I get this wire fixed, we need to tell Chase. Can you hold the broom while I find something to repair the hole?"

"Sure." She took the broom from him. As soon as he stepped away, the rooster flapped at the hole. But she kept him at bay.

Brock hurried back with a spool of wire and cutters. He threaded the wire to make a seam across the hole, with the rooster flogging the broom through the whole procedure. By the time the repair was finished, she was shaking.

"That should keep him." He raised up, took the broom from her. "Hey." His hands settled on her shoulders. "You okay?"

"I just don't know who would want to hurt Landry and Chase. She can't handle this."

"We won't tell her. But Chase has to know someone has it out for this place. Maybe he'll know who we're dealing with. Or it could be teenagers playing pranks. Whoever it is, we'll get to the bottom of it. And it'll be okay." He squeezed her hand.

Gentle, calloused palm. Soothing, comforting. And suddenly, the effect the cowboy's touch had on her was much more worrisome than dude ranch hijinks.

Chapter Four

❧

"We can't tell Landry about this." Chase paced the office.

"That's why we asked to talk to you alone." If only Brock could take away his friend's stress. But instead, he was adding to it.

"What about a competing dude ranch?" Devree picked at her nails. "Any owners capable of pulling something like this to steal business?"

"No. The other owners are stand up people. They might undercut our prices, but not purposely try to sabotage us. I can't imagine anyone I know doing this."

"Anyone got a bone to pick with you?" Brock pressed on. They had to figure this out. "An ex-employee maybe?"

Chase snapped his fingers. "There was a ranch hand. Nash Porter. I fired him shortly after Landry and I met. A real troublemaker."

"Is he still around these parts?" He glanced at Devree.

Fiddling with her phone? Was she trying to play it calm, ease Chase's worries?

"He's in jail." She caught his gaze.

"He is? How do you know?" Chase zeroed in on her.

"I just googled him. Assault and battery, stemming from a bar fight."

"I'm not surprised." Chase tunneled his fingers through his hair. "There's no one else I can think of. Here's what we're gonna do. Not a word to Landry. I'll have the locks changed for the cabin. Only y'all get keys. No one else."

"I'll change them out today."

"And I'm sorry about the rooster, Devree. He won't bother you again."

"I'm fine."

"You should have seen her. She handled him like a pro." Maybe she was tougher than she realized. And Brock was beginning to suspect she didn't hate the country as much as she thought she did. Trouble was—she'd probably never realize it.

Besides, his mom had toughed it out once. Then returned to the city just like Devree would.

"Come to supper with us tomorrow night, Brock. Landry's been wanting to have you join us."

"I reckon I'm always up for good grub."

"Six o'clock. But no talk of live traps or wire cutters or disgruntled saboteurs."

"My lips are sealed. But does that mean I can't tell about watching this one run from Rusty?"

Chase chuckled. "As long as you don't mention how he got out."

"I bet y'all wouldn't laugh if his spurs were aimed in your direction." Devree's cheeks went pink, but her good-natured smile revealed only affection for her brother-in-law.

"You're right." Chase sobered. "He could have easily hurt you."

"No harm done. Except for two years he shaved off my life expectancy." She stood. "We better get to work.

The hands are coming to move the old furniture out this morning."

"I emptied the interloper's live trap and reset both." He followed her lead. "Maybe the mouse population has decreased during our absence."

Devree closed her eyes for a second, then headed for the door. "Don't worry, Chase. We're on it. This wedding will go off without a hitch and the happy couple will have a pristine cabin ready for their honeymoon."

"I still think we should report it to the police." Brock adjusted his hat.

"No!" Chase cleared his throat. "It would get around town and Landry would hear of it for sure. Just keep an eye on things."

"Will do." Brock followed Devree out. The guy he'd chased into the woods worried him. But he wanted to keep an eye on Devree most of all. What if she'd gotten to the cabin first? Caught Ball-Cap in the act. He could have hurt her. Once they were outside, he grabbed her elbow.

She turned to face him with a puzzled frown. "What?"

"I'm going to the hardware store to get new locks. I don't want you going to the cabin alone."

"Trust me, I won't. Too many mice for my comfort." But her attempt to make light of the situation didn't disguise what he saw deep in her eyes.

Fear.

The dude ranch dining room was hopping with guests as the drone of multiple conversations filled the room. Typical Friday night. Devree sat in a secluded corner with Landry and Chase, as Brock gave a detailed recount of her bout with Rusty.

"I wish I could have seen it." Landry giggled. "I can't believe you got him back in the pen all by yourself."

Devree shrugged, as if her rooster wrangling was nothing. "You expected me to turn into a screaming ninny?"

"Well—yes."

It was good to hear her sister laugh, even if it was at her expense.

But then Landry frowned. "I wonder how he got out."

Devree's gaze met Brock's, then shifted to her brother-in-law.

"It doesn't matter how." Chase refolded his napkin. "It can't happen again. What if he'd gone after a guest? Or a child?"

"I guess you're right." Landry groaned. "But he's the prettiest rooster I've ever seen. I hate to part with him."

The kitchen doors opened and Chase's parents entered, headed their way with his chef dad carrying a covered roasting dish.

"What's this?" Landry's hand went to her chest. "I thought we were having buffet along with our guests."

"We always try our new dishes out on family." Chase's dad, Elliot, took the lid off with a flourish to reveal a large Thanksgiving-worthy turkey.

"Brock, I'm so glad you're back." Chase's mom, Janice, squeezed his shoulders. "We always thought the world of you. And your folks."

"Thanks. It's good to be back." There were so many mixed emotions on his face Devree wasn't sure she could keep up. A frown marred his brow, and she could tell his smile was forced. But his pale green eyes shone with happy memories. He seemed genuinely glad to be here, but jumpy as if he expected Becca to pounce on him at any minute.

"We'll leave you to your meal. I'll need honest opinions." Elliot wiped his hands on his apron, headed back to the kitchen, Janice trailing him.

"What were we talking about?" Landry frowned.

"Rusty." Chase picked up the large carving knife and fork, started to work on the bird. "I've already taken care of it. He won't bother anyone else around here."

Devree's gaze dropped to the bird as Chase made a deep slice across the breast. On it's back, all fours in the air. *Why would Elliot try a new turkey recipe so far away from Thanksgiving? Or was it Rusty?* Her eyes widened.

As Chase doled out slabs of meat, her appetite fled.

"Give me your plate, Devree." Chase held a large slice of meat between the carving set.

Mute, she shook her head.

"Are you okay? You look rather pale." Landry touched her hand.

"I can't eat him." Her vision clouded. He may have been mean, but she hadn't wanted him to die.

"Who?"

"I can't eat a rooster I knew by name."

Chase guffawed. "I can assure you, this isn't Rusty. It's turkey."

Her eyes met his. "You promise?"

"It's turkey." Landry squeezed her hand. "Rusty may be ornery, but he's much too pretty to eat. What did you do with him, Chase?"

"I gave him to the Whitlows. He's alive and well and far enough away you'll be able to sleep in tomorrow morning."

A relieved sigh whooshed out of her.

"Can I have your plate now?" Chase grinned.

She lifted her plate to accept the slice of meat as he lost his struggle with laughter. Again, at her expense. But she joined him. Soon Landry and Brock did too.

Appetite returned, she bowed her head as Chase prayed over the meal. Amens rounded the table and she muttered hers.

"The vegetables are on the buffet." Chase picked up his and Landry's plates, headed that way.

Devree caught Brock's gaze as she stood. She saw something different in his eyes—respect maybe?

Whatever it was made her pulse kick up a notch.

Dread weighed heavy on Brock's shoulders as he folded his napkin, set it by his plate. At least Chase and Landry hadn't harangued him about his mom during the meal. Or invited her to join them.

Though he'd have been more at ease if they hadn't included Devree. He couldn't seem to escape her presence and she always did a number on his peace of mind.

It was nice to see Chase's parents again. They'd always been such nice and welcoming folks. And the meal was mouthwatering. He thought of the moment Devree was sure the turkey was Rusty and almost lapsed into another bout of stomach-cramping laughter. How could a woman be so empathetic she didn't want to eat a rooster who'd tried to impale her?

"I don't mean to rush, but I need to get this lady back to her couch." Chase rose to his feet.

"Don't mind me." Brock picked up his hat, scooted his chair out. "That was the best meal I've had in some time. Is it always buffet here?"

"It depends on how many guests we have. When we're heavily booked, buffet is easier. I sure miss the kitchen." Landry stared longingly at the doors. "Your parents could probably use my help."

"They're fine." Chase scooped her up.

A few guests smiled; no one seemed to think it odd to see a pregnant woman carried out.

"I'll break your back." Landry giggled as Chase walked

toward the foyer with her cradled in his arms. "Hey, Brock, don't run off. Join us in the great room."

He'd have loved to come up with an excuse. He was afraid, despite their deal, they'd bring up his mother. For that matter, if he went back to his bunk, he could avoid running into her. But he worked for the Donovans. He couldn't really refuse their offer.

"Sure. I'll get the door." Brock opened the double doors into the lobby. Chase carried his wife through.

As Devree trailed them, she glanced back at Brock. Her rich blue dress matched her eyes, caused his breath to stutter.

Landry smacked Chase in the chest. "If I could eat laying down, you'd make me, wouldn't you?"

"Whatever it takes." The seriousness in his tone silenced her protests.

She patted her stomach. "We're fine. Don't worry."

He set her down—oh, so gently—on the couch. The care and love in his eyes reminded Brock of just what was at stake. Making the situation with his mother seem trivial.

"Happy Trails" started up, Chase's ringtone. He dug his phone from his pocket, sighed and turned it off.

"Who was it?"

"That real estate developer. You'd think as many times as I've rejected his call, he'd realize he's barking up the wrong tree. This place has been in my family for decades." Chase took his place at the end of the couch with Landry's feet in his lap. "How's the fishing cabin coming?"

Despite Chase's attempt to change the subject, Brock's brain was stuck on the real estate developer. Took him back to his days of hounding landowners during his short-lived and ill-fated business partnership.

"It's overrun with mice." Devree clamped a hand to her mouth, cut her gaze to Landry. "But we're handling it."

"I won't faint." Landry rolled her eyes. "I can handle the truth. I just don't understand where they're coming from. It's like somebody's trucking them in or something."

Devree's gaze met Brock's.

"I caulked all the plumbing, around the windows and doors, and underneath the baseboards and trim. With it airtight, we'll conquer them." And changed the locks so Ball-Cap couldn't bring in more. "We got the old furniture out today. That should help."

"I'm so glad you're here." Landry plumped her pillow. "I have to admit, I was getting worried."

"We'll have the cabin ready. I promise." Devree sat down in a cowhide wingback chair. "I got the curtains and bedspread today and the furniture will be here next week. I got some wall decor for the chapel too." Her focus went to the coffee table.

Brock settled in the matching chair and followed her gaze to an architectural magazine with a picture of him on the cover. An article from long ago. The city girl reporter had flirted with him mercilessly, tagging him "the cowboy carpenter," and made a big deal about him wearing a Stetson instead of a hard hat. He'd built luxury cabins for wealthy clients all over Texas back then. A lifetime ago.

"Why did you stop building your cabins?" Chase gestured to the magazine. "The article's quite impressive."

His mouth went dry. He didn't want to get into the fiasco with Phoebe. And her father. "I went into partnership, tried to go on a grander scale, but it didn't work out."

"I wish we could afford your cabins here." Landry rolled onto her side. "I'm afraid ours probably seem beneath you."

"They're cozy and perfect for a vacation. Besides, I'm happy to be here. To help out a friend." He was. He just wished he wasn't constantly distracted by Devree and her pretty blue eyes. And his mother lurking about somewhere on the premises weighed heavy on his mind. He stood. "I appreciate y'all inviting me to supper, but I think I'll turn in."

"Glad you could make it. Eat in the dining room anytime you like. On the house."

"I don't mind paying."

"We know. But you're getting us out of a major bind. The least we can do is feed you."

"Good night, then." He headed for the exit. The night sounds—frog's croaks, cricket's chirps, horse's whinnies—tugged at him. He'd sat on the porch swing many a night with his dad. He knew he should get going, back to his room. But as housekeeper, his mom should be long gone by now. He could sit a spell.

Closing his eyes, he settled on the swing. Old spice cologne and tales of the day's handyman chores filled his memory. His dad's calloused hands gentle, his voice low. Brock leaning his cheek on his dad's arm. He'd often fallen asleep in the swing, then awoken in his bed the next morning.

The door opened and he became instantly alert. Surely, not his mom. He stiffened, then quickly relaxed as Devree stepped outside. Gasping when she spotted him.

"Sorry, I didn't know you were out here."

"I didn't mean to be."

"I love sitting on the porch swing at night."

He scooted to the end, patted the slats beside him. "Feel free."

She hesitated a moment, but headed his way in the end. The swing barely shifted with her slight weight.

"I don't know why I like it out here." She shuddered. "There's probably snakes lurking. Or bats. Or bears for that matter. Maybe even a man with wire cutters. But I feel safe so close to the house and I love the night sounds. You don't get that in the city."

"I imagine not."

"And the stars are so bright here. So many of them."

He scanned the horizon, ashamed he often took the stars for granted. The black curtain sprinkled with sparkling flecks spread for miles. "So, why do you stay there?"

"It's where I belong. It's nice to visit the country—hear the sounds, experience the slowed-down lifestyle—but I could never live here. I'd be bored to tears."

Her statement was a good reminder. For a short time, they'd work together. Then they'd go their separate ways. "I could never live anywhere else."

"Do you think we put Landry's mind at ease? With my blurting out the mouse issue."

"She seemed relieved." The swing had almost stopped and he pushed off with his boot. "Just wish she wasn't right about someone trucking mice into the fishing cabin. Maybe I scared him off and the mice will be gone in the morning."

"Where do you even find so many mice?"

"Good question. Maybe the city dump."

"We should go there, ask around, see if anyone's been setting traps."

With the renewed swaying, a waft of apples caught his senses. "What are you, a detective?"

"I just want this craziness to end. If we don't get rid of the mice before the Brighton/Anderson wedding, it'll be a disaster."

"The cabin's caulked as tight as a storm shelter and the locks have been changed. I think the mice invasion is over."

"Maybe so. But if someone's trying to sabotage the dude ranch, they'll come up with another way. He broke into the cabin." The quiver in her voice tugged at him. "What if the ranch house is next?"

"The last thing we need is you playing amateur detective. We don't know what kind of person we're dealing with here. Leave it to Chase and me to ask questions or do any investigating. Understood?"

"Will you please talk Chase into calling the police?"

"I'll do my best." He pushed to his feet. "See you in the morning."

"First thing."

With all his worries over his friends and her reminder that she was a city girl through and through, why did he feel so pulled toward Devree? Despite the warm night, a chill settled in deep. He had absolutely nothing in common with her. He'd better tread carefully.

"Are they gone?" Devree peeked through the cracked door into the fishing cabin.

"There were five in the live trap and no extra traps." Brock scanned the living room. "I haven't seen any movement, so maybe."

Tentatively, she stepped inside, arms loaded with draperies.

"I told you I'd help with those." He grabbed the bundle from her with a grimace. "What is all this?"

His spicy cologne in her space. "Curtains."

"Men don't like curtains."

"Women do."

"Do they have to be flowered?"

"It's a honeymoon cottage."

"You're forgetting the cabin part. These timbers and caulking are rustic. You can't put flowered curtains up."

"This is shabby chic decor, which is considered rustic." She pulled up a picture on her tablet of floral wingback chairs paired with a cowhide rug against hardwood and log walls. "And you didn't complain about the ones in the bedroom."

"They're white and you can put as many cowhide rugs down as you want, but men don't like flowers." He wasn't being argumentative, just passionate.

"I can't do the whole place in white. It'll be—" she searched for the right word "—monotonous. Besides, Landry approved these curtains."

"Of course, she did. She's a woman. I bet Chase would balk if he saw them."

"You really think it's that important?"

"The wedding's all about the bride. The groom parades around in a penguin suit she picked out with a flower on his lapel and some girly-colored cockamamy vest." He covered his ears with both hands. "He's spent months hearing about bouquets, colors, cake flavors and designs. At least let him feel like a man in the honeymoon cottage."

Did his strong opinion on the subject come from experience? Had Brock been married? Whatever his story, his plea made sense. It really shouldn't be all about the bride.

"You know—you may have a point." She dug her phone out of her pocket, punched in Landry's number.

Her sister answered on the second ring. "Boredom 101 here."

"Hey, sis. Brock thinks the flowered curtains don't fit in the cottage and that I should try to incorporate male tastes too. What do you think?"

"That actually makes sense. But it can't be too manly. It's a honeymoon cottage."

"Agreed. But if we put our heads together, we could come up with a balance of feminine and masculine, so the bride and the groom will feel comfortable. Maybe Brock could go to Rustick's with me and give me some pointers."

He shook his head, held his palms toward her as if warding off a blow.

"I like that idea." Landry sounded entirely too pleased. Probably getting ideas about fixing her up with Brock. "Just don't go too masculine. No dead animals and such."

"I'll send you pictures of our choices, get your approval."

"I'll be here."

Devree ended the call.

"I don't shop."

"You're done caulking and Landry thought it was a great idea. And you'll love this store. It's all log furniture and deer antler chandeliers."

"And flowered curtains."

"We'll see what else she has. Landry's counting on you."

"You just had to throw that in there, didn't you?" He glanced down at the bundle of flowered curtains he held. "I reckon I'll go if it'll get these back where they came from."

"Come on, I'll drive."

"If it's all the same to you, I'd rather drive us in my truck."

"Whatever makes you feel manly."

With a chuckle, he followed her out, double-checked that the new lock clicked in place. Why had she suggested they ride together? They could have met at Rustick's in separate vehicles. Now she'd be stuck in his truck with him.

Him and his spicy cologne, enigmatic green eyes, cleft chin and dimples that came out of nowhere. What had she been thinking subjecting herself to all that in close quarters?

Chapter Five

Saturday morning in town meant extra car and human traffic—vehicles whizzed by and pedestrians clogged the sidewalk. Faded logs notched together at the corners lined the exterior of the store, large windows flanking the glass doors—Rustick's seemed like Brock's kind of place.

An older gentleman sat on a long church pew in front of the store, carving a walking stick with a knife.

"Why, Jed Whitlow—" Devree plopped down beside him "—you're just the guy I need to see."

Jed shot her a wink. "Why's that, Ms. Devree?"

"Does your grandson still work at the landfill?"

Brock's hackles went up. He nudged her foot with his, a subtle reminder she shouldn't be doing the detective-thing.

"Sure does." Jed puffed his chest up. "He's a senior in college. Almost got 'er wrapped up."

"This is my friend, Brock McBride. He's thinking about getting a pet boa constrictor."

Clever. Not what he'd expected. Brock relaxed a bit.

"Sweet. I've always wanted one, but the missus would move out if I came home with one."

"Marilyn is a wise woman." She laughed. "I was thinking if Brock gets his snake, he might be able to get free food for it from the landfill while taking care of an environmental issue at the same time. Do you think they'd let him bring a live trap to catch mice for the snake's supper?"

"I can check with him. I reckon Steven would have to ask his boss, but he could probably fix you up with rats yea big." Jed spread his hands apart ten inches or so. "I don't think anybody would mind getting rid of them."

She closed her eyes, for just a second. "Ask Steven. But make sure Brock wouldn't be cutting into anyone else's territory. There might be someone else catching rodents at the landfill to feed a pet snake."

"I doubt anybody else would ask. They'd probably just sneak on the property at night and set their traps."

"Tell Steven not to say anything to his boss just yet." Brock gave Jed an eye roll. "My girlfriend's not sold on it. But thanks for your help."

Jed's knowing gaze pinged back and forth between them. "Anytime."

"See you around." Devree waved.

Brock opened the door to Rustick's and she stepped inside.

"What did you go and do that for?" she whispered, punching him in the shoulder. "Now he thinks I'm your girlfriend."

"I didn't say that. I was just coming up with a reason the kid shouldn't say anything to his boss." He shrugged. "If it gets around that we're asking about live traps, our culprit might hear we're trying to track him down. And besides—" he waggled his eyebrows at her "—would it be so horrible to be my girlfriend?"

"We barely know each other, we have nothing in common and we're both only here for a short time."

His chest deflated. Though he'd been convincing himself of the same thing, using those same reasons, hearing them come from her, hurt. And now that he'd put the question out there and been shot down, he had to play it off as a joke. He clutched his heart in dramatic fashion. "You wound me, fair lady."

She huffed out a sigh, and he tried to focus on their surroundings as opposed to her obvious lack of interest.

Man-cave paradise greeted him. A treasure trove of log furnishings. More than Brock could take in. But not enough to keep his mind off of Devree's words.

A slender woman stepped toward them with two little girls.

"Hi, Brock."

He looked down. Ruby. His gaze bounced up to the woman. Long light brown hair, kind gray eyes.

"I'm Scarlet Miller." She stuck her hand out and he clasped it. "I'm so glad you're here." Her smile was genuine. "I mean in Bandera."

"Thanks." He tried to keep it casual.

"This is my friend, Cheyenne." Ruby fought for his attention.

"Hi, Cheyenne." He glanced down at the dark-haired child with her.

"Come give me a hug before you go." A brunette woman scurried from the back of the store, knelt to Cheyenne's level. "You be good and use your best manners."

"We always enjoy having her." Scarlet took both girls by the hand, but her interest returned to him. "Well, we won't keep you. But maybe you could come over for supper while you're here. I'd love for you to meet Drew, my husband."

"Thanks for asking. We'll see." Code for no. But a kinder way of putting it. "Nice meeting you." He opened the door for them.

"You too." Scarlet tugged the girls outside as Ruby waved goodbye.

"You brought the curtains back." The brunette sounded as if she'd expected it.

Devree introduced Brock and his position at the dude ranch. "He's helping get the fishing cabin ready for our honeymooners. He doesn't think the groom will like flowered curtains."

"I tried to tell you." The brunette propped her hands on her hips.

"You did. I should have listened." Devree turned to him. "This is Resa McCall, Landry's neighbor, friend, Rustick's owner and furniture designer."

"Your little girl looks just like you."

"Actually, she's my niece. But I just got engaged to her father." She winced. "It's not as weird as I just made it sound."

Sounded as complicated as his life. He'd just met his stepsister for the first time, though she'd been part of his family for twelve years.

"I'm behind." Devree grabbed Resa's left hand, inspected the sparkler gracing her ring finger. "When did this happen?"

"Just last weekend." Resa flashed a smile even brighter than the diamond. "Anyway, it's nice meeting you, Brock. What are we looking for?"

"Something not too feminine, not too masculine. A nice balance of both." Devree scanned the store.

"I've got the perfect thing. We just got a new line in from Dallas, the Burlap-and-Lace collection." Resa led them to the left side of the store where numerous draperies hung.

A few flowers, but mostly wildlife and horse designs. Devree must have worked hard to find the ones she'd bought.

"We have four different designs." Resa pulled curtains from the display rods, held one up for them to see.

Brock grimaced at the large burlap panel lined by a wide strip of lace. "Still too frilly. No offense."

"None taken." Resa held up the next choice.

"Too burlap." Devree shot down the panel with a thin band of lace.

"Next." Resa held up another.

"Not bad." Brock inspected the curtain, intermixed with broad strips of burlap and narrow lace. No flowers or ruffles.

"You could feel like a man with these?"

"They're tolerable."

"Good." Devree smiled. "I like them too."

"I didn't say I liked them. If it were up to me, I'd say no curtains."

"Good thing it's not up to you. Let's see the last choice."

Resa held up another curtain, glancing back and forth between them with a grin that said she knew something they didn't.

Burlap with a ruffle at the top and a band of white at the bottom with holes in it.

"Oh, I love the eyelet trim at the hem," Devree gushed. "These would be great in the kitchen. And maybe the bathroom. Do they come in café style?"

"They do. And I have a shower curtain to match."

"What do you think?" Devree turned to him.

"Bearable." Though he felt his man card slipping a bit out of reach.

She rolled her eyes.

"What? I like them better than the flowery ones you brought back."

"Okay, I'll take the mix for the living room and the eyelet for the bathroom and kitchen."

For the next several minutes, the two women dug through the shelves to find the right size for each curtain, then stacked their finds in Brock's arms.

"So how's Landry?" Resa's brow furrowed.

"Bored to tears. But I think her stress level is down since Brock showed up and the cabins are coming along nicely."

"I wish I had more time to spend with her. But with the store and my designs, my hunky fiancé and now a wedding to plan…" Resa sighed. "There just isn't enough time in the day."

"She knows you've got a lot going on."

"But I shouldn't be too busy for my dearest friend. Hey, I know—we need to set up a meeting for wedding planning."

"Do you have a date in mind?"

"We're hoping for the third weekend in June."

"This June?"

"Please tell me you're available. Do not make me wait any longer to marry that man of mine."

Brock strolled through the store as the ladies hashed out their schedules. Why couldn't he have someone to love, someone who couldn't wait to marry him? Because he kept going after the wrong women.

Despite his mother's abandonment and Phoebe dumping him, he'd always longed for a family of his own. One like he'd had before his father's passing.

"Okay, got you on my calendar." But the smile Devree gave her friend wasn't real. She obviously, truly wasn't into weddings anymore. Why? He'd like to know what had soured her on her chosen profession. Though he couldn't dwell on why he cared.

"Let's do our wedding discussing at the dude ranch with

Landry included. I mean, she is my maid of honor." Resa checked her phone. "What about May 18?"

"She'd love that." Devree grabbed Resa's hand, gave it a squeeze. "Let's surprise her. But wait. You want to meet on May 18 to plan a wedding for June 16?"

"We don't want all the hullabaloo. As long as I have my groom and a photographer, I'll be happy. And Landry's holding the great room at the dude ranch and the dining room for me on that date."

"Okay, lunch on the eighteenth."

"Sounds great." Resa added more packages to Brock's pile of burlap. "That should do it. Take these to the counter for me."

Brock did as he was told and Resa bagged the curtains. How had this become his life—shopping for curtains and wedding discussions? By hanging out with a city-girl wedding planner, that's how. He could suffer through it for Chase and Landry.

"These actually cost a little less than the floral draperies. I'll figure out the difference and send Chase the updated invoice."

"Thanks, Resa. See you on the eighteenth."

Brock grabbed both enormous bags, opened the door for Devree.

"I can take one of those."

"I've got them." He hurried to stash the bags in the back seat of his cab. By the time he climbed into the driver's seat, she was already in. "Getting hot." He started the engine, turned the air on full blast and maneuvered into the flow of traffic on Main Street.

"I'm glad we did this. The new curtains fit the cabin much better than the ones I originally chose. Thanks to you, hundreds of grooms will be happier." The last bit held a note of sarcasm.

"What do you have against grooms?"

"It's not so much the grooms." She closed her eyes. "It's the whole wedding thing."

"But you're a wedding planner."

"Event planner." Her gaze went past him, off into the distance. "It's more the marriage part that gets me. They don't seem to last."

"Some do." He stopped at the only red light. "So how'd you get into wedding planning, then?"

She huffed out a sigh. "Once upon a time, I was a romantic."

"But not anymore?"

"I went to my first wedding when I was twelve. My mom's cousin." A wistful lilt hung in her words. "Lace and flowers everywhere. I decided I wanted to spend my life creating stunning weddings. Making perfect days for brides without going overboard, without breaking the bank. Just a simple, beautiful day to remember and begin a marriage."

"What happened?"

"By the time I was putting together my fifth wedding, my second and third couples were filing for divorce." Her shoulders sagged. "After eight years, my divorce rate is at forty percent."

"That's not your fault. Focus on the sixty."

"I try." She lifted one shoulder. "But it's so discouraging. And I'm so jaded. Each wedding I plan now, I expect them to crash and burn in a few years. Or months. I just go through the motions."

"And never take the chance on love for yourself."

She met his gaze. "I don't see a ring on your finger."

"I haven't found the right girl." The right *country* girl.

"I hope it works out for you, but I wouldn't hold my breath."

"I know lots of happy couples. Look at Landry and Chase."

"Yes." She rolled her eyes. "But the first jerk she fell for dumped her at the altar. She had to get her heart broken before she met Chase."

"Still, she found him."

"Only after heartbreak." The dullness in her tone said she'd been there as well.

"Ever wonder if you're missing out?"

"No." She hugged herself. "I just want to get the Brighton/Anderson wedding done, see my niece or nephew born healthy and get back to my life. In Dallas." She sighed. "But now I'll have to come back for Resa's ceremony. At least it sounds simple and small."

The light turned green and he gassed it through the intersection.

"What about Resa's fella? Think they'll make it?"

"I've only met him in passing. I hope so."

Phoebe had left a bitter taste in his mouth for love. But seeing Chase and Landry so happy gave him hope. And spending his days with the plucky wedding planner— turned decorator and aspiring event planner—had him thinking about a future he had no business entertaining. Especially not with her thoughts on love and her determination to get back to her beloved Dallas.

Devree peeked in the great room. Landry lay on the couch, flipping through a magazine with Chase nowhere in sight. She'd dreaded Sunday all week. For the first time since arriving in Bandera, she was on the rotation to go to church this morning. Maybe she could get out of it by offering to stay with Landry while Chase went.

"Hey, sis." She bustled into the room, sat in the wing-back across from Landry's couch.

"Why aren't you getting ready?"

"For what?"

"Church. You're on the rotation this morning."

The Donovan family her sister had married into had been encouraging employees to take turns attending church services for years. "I thought I'd sit with you and let Chase go."

"No one needs to sit with me. It's only an hour. I'd love to go and I won't let you miss your chance."

"I really don't want to leave you here alone."

"I'm not alone. There are several of the staff here. And the chapel is a hop, skip and a jump away."

"I'd rather stay with you."

Landry's gaze narrowed. "Why don't you want to go?"

She'd have to spill. But Landry didn't need to stress over her spiritual condition. Or a reminder of the reason. "It's been a while since I've been to church."

Landry looked at her quizzically. "Why?"

She couldn't let her sister know she hadn't been to church since seeing that tiny coffin.

A childhood hang up surfaced and she decided to go with that. "When we were teenagers, Mom and Dad planned all those wonderful family vacations and outings. But then some employee would get sick or quit, and we didn't get to go." A wave of guilt washed over her, but Landry didn't need to hear the truth.

"But you must realize that sick employees or unreliable ones aren't God's fault. That's just part of owning a business. And we got to spend plenty of time with Mom and Dad by tagging along to the store with them."

"I know. And as an adult, I realize how important the Christian bookstore is. They're getting to be almost extinct. But I figure after all this time of me being mad at

Him and ignoring Him—" she ducked her head "—God must be done with me."

"Oh, Devree, how could you think that? God never gives up on anyone. He's just waiting for you to stop ignoring Him. All you have to do is ask for forgiveness. He's waiting right where you left Him."

Something inside her chest squeezed.

"When I moved here, after my first engagement ended so publicly, I was so mad and bitter I hadn't been to church in a while. But Chase's mom talked me into attending and all that anger began to melt."

"Last year, after our baby died, I thought I'd die too." Landry's chin trembled. "But God got me through it. Please don't try to wade through this world without Him."

Devree's vision blurred. What right did she have to be mad at God over Landry's tragedy, while her sister had chosen to lean on Him more fully?

"I won't. Not anymore." She swiped at a tear she hadn't even realized had fallen and stood. "I better go get ready."

Even though she hadn't told her sister the truth, she'd acknowledged it to God. And He'd heard her silent torment. She hurried up the stairs.

I'm sorry, God. I didn't have any right to get mad at You or ignore You. And it stops now. Peace replaced the pressure in her chest and suddenly she couldn't wait to get to church.

Brock was here at Chase's insistence. He wanted to be here. In the chapel on Sunday morning. But what if his mom was on this service's rotation schedule? He couldn't relax, and church should be the one place he could.

From his vantage point in the back pew, he could see that ranch employees and a smattering of guests made up the congregation. No sign of her. If he'd known she wasn't coming, he'd have chosen a closer pew.

Devree sat with Chase about halfway up. Looking way too pretty in her vivid purple dress.

Third row from the front, a child leaned over the back of the pew, staring at him. Ruby, with her hair done up in red ribbons. His gaze went to the woman beside her. Light brown hair, wavy. Slender shoulders. Scarlet. She whispered something to Ruby. The child promptly turned around and sat facing forward.

The man beside Ruby wore a typical western shirt, his arm across the back of the pew, hand on Scarlet's shoulder. Must be the husband, Drew. What were their supper conversations like these days? Did they discuss the black sheep stepbrother holding a grudge against dear sweet Becca? How had she managed to make him the bad guy when it had been all her?

At least she wasn't with them.

A thick, stocky man with a ruddy complexion stepped onto the stage behind the pulpit. "Good morning." Booming voice, perfect for preaching. "We're so glad you could be here with us. Turn to page fifty-four in your hymn book."

The piano started up—"I'll Fly Away." The old standard from his childhood brought a rush of good memories. Until he got that odd feeling. Someone was staring at him. He scanned the crowd.

Everyone seemed to be facing forward or looking at their hymn book and it wasn't the preacher. Brock's gaze went to the piano player.

His mom.

The words to the hymn stifled in his throat.

She gave him a tentative smile before her gaze went back to her music.

From adoring mom, to grief-stricken and neglectful, to drug addict, to remarried, stepmom, church pianist. His mom had certainly come full circle.

He didn't hear anything after that. None of the following hymns. None of the sermon. The man in front of him stood and he realized it was over. Down to the closing hymn and altar call. He rose to his feet as several people went up to the front, including Devree. The piano stopped, but the congregation kept singing. His mom descended the stage steps. He stiffened.

Would she approach him, make a scene? She knelt at the altar and he started breathing again.

The song wound down as people returned to their pews. Someone said a closing prayer. He was almost first out the door.

Heavy footfalls behind him. "Brock. Wait." The preacher.

Reluctantly, he stopped, turned around. "How do you know my name?"

The preacher's ruddy complexion was even redder with his exertion. "Ron Fletcher." He stuck his hand out and Brock clasped it. "I'm your, uh…your mama's husband."

Add preacher's wife to his mom's circle. He wanted to pull his hand away. But his manners wouldn't allow it.

"Look, son, I don't know what your relatives told you about your mama to turn you against her."

If this guy knew the truth, would he still be pleading her case?

"She's a good woman. Loves the Lord. Loves you like nobody's business. Cried many a night over you. Days too—like now. All worried you'll leave without talking to her."

"I'm staying until Chase finds someone else. Only because he's a friend and he needs me. But I don't think we have anything to discuss."

"Do me a favor?"

"Can't promise anything." Brock shoved his hands in his pockets.

"Give her a chance."

"Can't promise anything," he repeated and turned away.

"Just think about it."

How could he work here and continue to avoid his mother? Tell her to keep her distance or he'd bust her secret wide open? He wasn't into blackmail. But if he let her think he was, maybe that would keep her at bay.

He climbed in his truck, desperate for escape. But as he slowly maneuvered through the parking lot, past the church to the exit, he noticed Ruby standing at the glass door. Eyes locked on his, she waved.

Chapter Six

"Could you move it this way a bit?" Devree directed the Rustick's delivery guys on where to put the new couch. "Perfect. Thanks. And that's everything." She signed the work order, verifying she'd received each piece and the men left.

It was the last day of April, the week of the wedding. She was starting to feel the stress as the countdown to Saturday's nuptials began. Could they get everything ready in time? With some nut, trucking in mice?

"At least it's not flowery." Brock surveyed the furnishings.

"I thought the white fabric would brighten it up in here. I picked these up too." She placed a burlap-and-lace throw pillow at each end of the couch. "Can you help me hang the wall art?"

"At your service."

"This, centered above the fireplace." She held up the rustic window with four divided panes of glass to show him the right height, then stood back out of his way.

He used his drill to sink the screw and hung the window.

"What do you think?" She surveyed the piece. Curvy

wooden letters painted pale aqua spelled out *Mr.* and *Mrs.* in catty-cornered panes of the window. A nice pop of color.

"The peeling paint of the frame balances the girly blue color. It's tolerable."

"This must be hard for you. From building designer cabins to seeing others doing the building while you end up playing interior decorator with me."

"I don't mind. Keeps me busy."

From the looks of that fancy magazine, he was quite talented. Not the country bumpkin she'd pegged him as at all. Humble and willing to put everything aside to help his friend. Appealing character traits. Not to mention the cute cowboy thing he had going.

"I'd like this over here." She picked up a galvanized windmill clock, held it where she wanted it. "Can you hold this and let me look from a distance?"

"Now, this I like. Nothing girly about it." He held it for her.

She took a few steps back. "A little lower and to the left. Right there."

Brock marked the spot, drove the screw into the wall.

"The great thing about logs, you don't have to worry about finding a stud."

"I saw you in church yesterday." He hung the windmill. "Guess we're on the same rotation."

"I think it swaps around." Should she broach the subject? It wasn't technically discussing his mother. "This was my first week to be on the rotation. I knew Ron was a military chaplain, but I missed the memo about him being the preacher here. If I'd known, I'd have warned you."

"He clued me in. I don't want to talk about it. What's next?"

Should have kept her mouth shut. "I thought this wreath would look nice here. It's made of vines from Grapevine,

Texas and the cotton is grown locally too." She placed it on the wall where she wanted.

"Rustick's has some cool stuff." He took it from her.

She moved back. "To the right and lower. Perfect."

As he marked the spot, the door opened.

Devree turned around. Becca. Her breath stalled.

Brock glanced over, did a double take. "What are you doing here?"

"I was supposed to vacuum before the new furniture arrived." She looked around, bit her lip. "Guess I'm too late. But that's okay, I can move it and clean underneath."

"You know..." Devree tapped her chin with an index finger, as if she were thinking. "There was a clock made from a wooden electric spool at Rustick's. It would be perfect in the kitchen. I think I'll go back and get it. Maybe you can help Becca move the furniture?"

His mouth gaped, eyes begging her to stay.

"See you in a bit." Ignoring his silent plea, she backed out the door and shut it. She really had been thinking she should have gotten the other clock—but it could have waited. The conversation between mother and son, on the other hand, was a long time coming. Devree's legs shook as she got in her car. He'd be mad at her. But she cared about him—not in a romantic way, of course—about his well-being. Brock needed the only parent he had left, whether he realized it or not.

"How are you?"

"Busy." Brock bit the words out. "Five minutes and I'm out of here."

"Fair enough." She smiled sadly and said nothing more as she got the vacuum cleaner out of the closet.

Thoughts of bolting for the door tumbled in his gut, but the many questions he had running through his head prevailed. "Why are you here?" He splayed his hands. "I remember you badgering Dad—trying to get him to move. Before he was even cold in the ground, you dragged me to your beloved Dallas."

She jerked, as if he'd struck her. "I moved because I couldn't face the memories of your father here."

"But you obviously can now."

"I've learned a lot." Mom shrugged. "The city isn't all I thought it was and you can't run from problems. That's part of how I ended up—"

"On drugs. Abandoning your son."

"I didn't abandon you."

"You never picked me up from the babysitter."

"I was just so lost without your father. I wanted an escape." She covered her face with both hands.

"I guess I was a reminder of him you decided you could do without."

"No." She shook her head. "I never meant to leave you."

"But you did."

"No." She pressed her knuckles against trembling lips. "I'm ashamed to admit it." She closed her eyes. "I forgot where I left you."

"Forgot?" A twitch started up in his jaw muscle. "How could you forget where you left your kid?" he roared.

She jumped, tears streaming again. "Drugs." She lifted one shoulder. "I was so messed up and Mrs. Simons was a new sitter. I couldn't remember where her house was. And by the time I came down and could remember, I knew if I went to get you, they'd arrest me."

"So you just left me there?" He'd imagined she hadn't wanted him. That she'd have more money for drugs without him. Never that she'd forgotten where he was. People forgot where they left things. Their eyeglasses, their keys, their phone. Not kids. Not kids they loved, anyway.

"Mrs. Simons was a nice lady and I was such a mess. I figured you were better off with her." Her chin wobbled. "But I never forgot about you. I missed you so badly—as if I'd cut off a piece of myself."

"Not enough to come back for me."

"I wanted to. So much." Her voice broke. "You'll never understand unless you've been on drugs. I wanted my next fix more. And I knew if I went to jail, there wouldn't be another. I've been clean for fifteen years. You can ask my former parole officer if you don't believe me."

So in the end, she had chosen drugs over him. "Why didn't you try to find me?"

"You were a teenager by the time I got myself together, and I figured you hated me." Her chin trembled. "With just cause." Her cheeks reddened. "I got caught—ended up in jail—got parole by agreeing to enter a faith-based rehab program. I accepted Jesus as my Savior. Are you a Christian?"

"Yes." Thanks to Mama Simons. She was the one he should consider his mom. The best of his foster families— until Pop Simons's mother was diagnosed with Alzheimer's and Brock had to give up his room.

"Oh good." She let out a sigh.

"I'll move the couch and leave you to your cleaning."

"Please wait." She blocked his path. "Tell me about your life. I prayed so hard for you to have a good one. Hoped the Simons would adopt you."

He glared at her. "Didn't happen. She called child services the second day you didn't show and arranged to be my guardian, then went through the process to foster me. Until Grandma needed to move in. After that, I bounced from foster home to foster home. Some ditched me because I cried myself to sleep every night, some because they decided they wanted a dog instead of a kid. Eventually, I aged out of the system and I've been on my own since."

"I'm so sorry." Her voice took on a breathy quality. "But you built a successful business. Are you married?"

"No." He'd fallen for a girl in Austin once, almost married her, until she reminded him not to trust city girls. "How did you end up back here?"

"Once I got out of the program, no one would hire me. So I came back. Partly for a job, partly because I thought you might show up some day." She clasped the vacuum again. "Chase's grandmother was still alive then and let me have my old position back. I married Ron twelve years ago."

She nibbled her lip. "He's a wonderful man, as much in the dark about me as everyone else. I know I should have been truthful. But I was so ashamed and Granny said no one else needed to know. And once I started falling for Ron, I was so afraid he wouldn't love me if he knew everything. That he wouldn't want an ex-addict near his daughter."

"You better get back to work, so I can. Have Chase call me when you've finished." He moved the couch away from the wall, then bent to flip the vacuum she held on, effectively ending the conversation.

Her mouth opened, shut as the whine of the cleaner drowned out whatever she wanted to say.

He'd heard enough, anyway. It satisfied him immensely to walk out on her and slam the door.

Devree hesitated on the porch of the fishing cabin. Two hours had passed. Was Becca gone? Had she and Brock reconciled? Or had it out?

The door swung open. Brock stood there, grim-faced. "Don't ever do that to me again."

"I needed to get the clock. It's in the car. Kind of heavy. Can you—?"

"It could have waited." He stepped aside, ushered her in. *True.* "But I wanted to get the kitchen done today. So how did it go? Did you and Becca talk?"

"Enough. If she ever shows up again, do not try to manipulate a reunion between us. If I ever decide I want to work things out with her, I'll do it. On my terms. And timing."

"Okay. I get it. I'm sorry. I was only trying to help." *Subject closed.*

"Just don't. I'll get the clock from your car, so we can get back to work." He hurried out the door.

She stared after him. How could she fix this? How were they supposed to work together if he was all mad and stiff?

The door opened and Brock strode in carrying the massive clock. Chase just a few steps behind him.

"Wow, this place is different." Chase looked around, a hint of sadness in his eyes.

"Don't worry." Devree hurried to reassure him. "All your grandfather's things are at the new house. What do you think?"

"I guess you had to girly it up some, but it's not too bad."

"So you approve?"

"Not too shabby. You've done a fine job."

"Brock was a big help. I initially picked floral curtains and throw pillows."

Brock gave no reaction to her praise. Still frowning, he focused on Chase.

"Nice save, Brock." Chase stepped into the kitchen, then the bedroom. "I just wanted to see the final result. And Landry wants me to take pictures."

"I think the mice are a thing of the past, thankfully."

She rushed to cover Brock's silence. "While you're here, let me run an idea by you."

"What's that?" Chase took several pictures of the furnishings with his phone.

"I've been thinking of ways to promote my event planning when I get back to Dallas. I came up with a contest to bolster my services and then I thought of using the dude ranch as a venue. I could do a massive publicity campaign and have a drawing for a free company retreat here. With me as the event planner."

"After the baby?" Chase lowered his phone.

"Yes. You'd get publicity from the contest and retreat attendees would rent rooms. I can probably get florists and caterers I've worked with to donate services in exchange for exposure."

"Sounds feasible. I'll run it by Landry. And Mom and Dad might want to do the catering themselves."

"Great."

"My work is done here." Chase pocketed his phone. "I can't tell you what a load you've taken off Landry's mind, working together on this. She'll love what you did with the place."

"It's been kind of fun." Devree surveyed the room with pride. "I've never done anything like this, but we make a good team." She tried for eye contact with Brock, but he looked away.

Obviously, it wasn't fun for him. Not anymore, anyway.

Chase's gaze bounced from her to Brock. "You two getting along okay?"

"Well enough," Brock mumbled.

"Thanks for helping us out on this." Chase squeezed her shoulder, shook Brock's hand. "I know it's not really in either of your job descriptions."

"We've made it work," she promised.

Another curious glance between them and Chase left. "Where do you want the clock?" All business. None of the warmth he'd shown Chase. Or the teasing connection they'd shared before she'd meddled in his mom situation.

"On the wall behind the kitchen table."

He stalked into the kitchen, obviously eager to wrap this up and escape her for the rest of the day.

Somehow, him being mad at her didn't sit well. As if she'd lost something...special.

Devree took the stairs two at a time down to the foyer, peeked in the great room. No Landry. She must be still asleep.

She had a meeting with the bride and groom at the bakery in town that shouldn't take long. Typical bride, considering a flavor change at the last minute. Miranda would probably end up sticking with her original choice.

After the cake consultation, she had a few finishing touches to make at the fishing cabin. And a tense cowboy to try to soothe. Maybe he'd be better today.

She slipped on her sunglasses and stepped outside. Cows. She gasped, clasped a hand to her chest. Half a dozen cows. Surrounding her car. Two of them licking her passenger windows.

Wearing a mustard yellow sundress and heels, she wasn't clad for herding cattle. Nor did she have time. And she wasn't a fan of getting up close and personal with cows. They were big and stinky, and she liked them a lot better when they were behind a fence.

But she couldn't bother Chase with this. And no one else was about. Yet, even if she could get them away from her car, she couldn't just leave them out.

At least they weren't longhorns. She drew in a deep

breath, stepped purposely off the porch, waving her arms. "Shoo, shoo. Go back where you came from."

All six red-and-white faces turned her way. One bawled at her, but they didn't move. Two went back to licking her passenger side windows, leaving slimy tongue streaks from top to bottom.

"Shoo, shoo. Get back in your fence." She ran at them, but they paid her no mind. So she tried jumping up and down, waving her arms more frantically. "Come on, you stupid cows. I don't have time for this."

"Whoa. How'd they get out?" Brock rounded the ranch house.

"I don't know. They were just here when I came out."

"I'll get a feed bucket." He hurried toward the barn.

Within minutes, he returned with a pail full of grains. One of the cows bawled, then headed in his direction. The others followed.

Brock backed to the gate, opened it, led the cows inside. Once all six were back in the fence, he fastened it.

"Thanks." She got in her car, started the engine. But the passenger windows were a streaky mess she couldn't see through. She jumped out, hurried toward the ranch house.

"Where are you going?" Brock jogged toward her. "I thought you had a meeting."

"I need something to wipe their slobber off with. I can't see out my passenger side."

"Get in your car. I'll take care of it." He rushed to his truck, came back with a spray bottle and blue paper towels. Quickly, he sprayed the window down and wiped it clear. "Go."

"Thanks. Again." She gave him her best smile, waved goodbye.

At least he wasn't so mad at her that he wouldn't come

to her rescue. Maybe she'd offer to pay to have his cape dry-cleaned this time.

Five minutes later, she entered the bakery with time to spare.

"Devree." Miranda was as giddy as ever, with Joel's arm around her waist. If he couldn't care less about the wedding, he sure was putting on a good front.

"I hope you haven't been waiting long."

"Not at all. And you're early, anyway."

"Have a seat and I'll be with you in just a few." The owner waited on another customer.

"Thank you both for coming." Devree followed them to a table. "This is usually the most fun wedding prep meeting for the groom. Lots of cake flavors to taste. And you get to do it again."

"I've truly enjoyed all of it." Joel never took his eyes off Miranda. "It's meant I've gotten to spend time with the love of my life."

"Aww, isn't he sweet?" Miranda pressed her cheek against his. "Do you think we could see the honeymoon cottage since we're here? And maybe I could see those glass bell decorations you told me about."

"Sure." It was clean and ready minus a few wall decor items. And, hopefully, still mouse-free.

The couple stole a quick kiss.

And for some reason, this time, instead of gagging over their head-over-heels in love antics, Devree longed for what they had.

Brock reread the text from Devree.

Are you at the cabin? If so, is anything amiss? My bride and groom would like to see it while they're in town.

He'd replied that everything was fine. That didn't necessarily mean he had to stay. So, why was he still here? Because he didn't have anything else to do at the moment? He'd repaired the hole in the fence where the cows had gotten out. Reported the bad news to Chase—another fence cut. Adding to Chase's stress instead of detracting from it. He suggested it was time to call the police. His friend had promised to think about it.

In the meantime, one carpentry crew was hard at work completing the new house, another tackling the new honeymoon cottages and a demolition team was tearing down the old storm shelter by the chapel.

Sometimes he missed getting his hands dirty. This handyman gig wasn't enough to keep his mind busy. *Off of Devree.* Even with a fence-tampering vandal on the loose, he couldn't stop thinking about her. Despite their complete incompatibility and her interference with his mom yesterday, he was eager to spend the rest of his day with her. What was wrong with him?

He opened the door when he heard voices coming his way. Devree and the couple.

The sun set her hair on fire. The pretty mustard yellow sundress only accented her beauty.

"This is Brock, the handyman. And this is Miranda and Joel."

He forced his attention away from her and concentrated on the couple. He shook hands with Joel as they stepped up on the porch. "Nice to meet you."

"So is the cabin new?" Miranda frowned at the aged logs.

"It belonged to the owner's grandfather, but we recently updated the interior."

"Farmhouse decor." Miranda clapped her hands together. "I love it. It's so pretty."

"But still rustic. I like all the burlap." Joel looked around the living room.

Brock caught her gaze, gave her the tiniest smirk.

Her eyes narrowed. "You can thank Brock for that. I picked floral fabrics, but he gave me insight on the male perspective."

Nice. She gave credit where it was due. "I'll let you handle the rest of the tour. Good meeting y'all, and I'm glad you like what we've done here." He tipped his hat, headed out. He needed some air and to stop liking her so much.

"You like her, don't you?"

Brock stiffened at his mom's voice behind him. Definitely none of her business. He turned around, scowl firmly in place. "Who?"

"Devree. She's a sweet girl."

"Even if I did, she's too city."

"Opposites attract. Like your father and me. We made a great team."

"Our memories don't exactly line up. I remember you complaining about living on the ranch and causing arguments."

"All couples disagree sometimes." She leaned her elbows against the goat pen. "Your father and I loved each other. I was young and didn't appreciate this place then. But even with our issues, we were great together. You and Devree are too. I've watched you with her. You light up like a Texas sunrise when she's around."

"So, you're stalking me?"

"You make it sound so ominous. I can't help being drawn to my own flesh and blood."

He looked past her toward the barn. A cowhand turned away. Gossip traveled fast on a large ranch They were probably the hot topic at the moment.

"Please come to the chapel with me. Just to talk. Just for a minute."

He sighed. Might as well escape prying eyes. And besides, he had a feeling his mom wouldn't quit until he heard her out.

Chapter Seven

With the happy couple back on the road, Devree climbed up to the chapel loft carrying a box of glass bells.

The loft brimmed with lace, tulle and every other embellishment she'd accumulated over the years. She plopped down on the floor crisscross style. As she rewrapped the fragile bells in packing paper, she heard the chapel door open, then two sets of footfalls before the door closed.

Her hands stilled. Maybe someone had come to pray. The sanctuary was open at all times and she'd been instructed that if she was decorating and guests arrived, she should leave them in peace.

But clambering down the ladder wouldn't be very peaceful. Staying put and quiet was best.

"We have nothing to talk about." Brock's words came out gruff.

Devree's jaw dropped.

"Please, Brock, I just want to spend time with you," Becca pleaded. "To get to know the man you've become."

"With no help from you."

Devree's face steamed. She shouldn't be hearing this. On the other side of the two rooms in the loft, a door led to an empty area with an open air window for pictures. Maybe she could bail without breaking a leg.

"I'm sorry I wasn't there when you were a child." Becca's voice broke. "When you needed me most. But I'm here now. Can't we build a relationship?"

"I'm not interested. As soon as Chase hires another handyman, I'm out of here."

He'd lost his father at the tender age of eight and had a falling out with his mother in the years since. His aloneness drew her to him. Made her hurt for him. The one thing she could always count on was family. How did people without that bond get through life's hard knocks?

Lord, help Brock and Becca repair their past hurts. Find their way back to each other. Thankfully, she'd repaired her relationship with God last Sunday. She knew for certain that He heard her now.

"I didn't come here to see you, and I'm not staying for you." Brock's angry tone jarred her from her prayer.

"Please, can't you forgive me?"

Silence echoed. Tension swirled. Devree looked at the door that led to the loft window. Maybe she could make it. A broken leg would be better than this.

"If you don't keep your distance," Brock growled, "I won't keep your secret."

"That will only work for so long." Becca sniffled. "I'm trying to work up the courage to tell Ron the truth. And eventually, I will. Until then, I'll respect your wishes."

"You do that."

The door closed.

Brock spewed out a sigh.

Okay, leave now. Stop this torment. Knowing there was a secret. Things she shouldn't know. And her right foot was going to sleep.

There was a movement near her knee. The glass bell

rolled a slow circle, rustling the tissue paper. It got close to the edge of the stairwell. *Please stop!* If she reached for it, there would be more tissue rustling. In slow motion the bell reached the edge, teetered. And fell.

She closed her eyes in anticipation but there was no sound. No glass breaking. Impossible. She opened her eyes, leaned over to peer through the opening.

A large hand held the bell. "What are you doing up there?" Brock snarled.

"I'm sorry. I didn't mean to—Miranda asked to see the bells before they left. I was just putting them away when y'all came in." She scooted closer.

Stormy eyes as green as a prickly pear cactus met hers. "And decided to eavesdrop instead of letting us know you were there."

"I didn't know who came in. I thought it might be some-one coming to pray, so I decided to be quiet and not dis-turb them." She stood, brushed the seat of her dress off. "I'll leave you alone. I can do this later." She descended the stairs, dreaded facing him.

At the bottom, she kept her gaze averted, started to sidestep him.

But he blocked her. Like a wall.

She slowly met his glower. "Before I forget to tell you, I saw Jed in town as I was leaving the bakery. His grand-son doesn't know of anyone ever setting live traps at the landfill."

"For the record, I'm not blackmailing her." He closed his eyes. "I have no intention of telling anyone anything. I just want her to leave me alone."

"This is none of my business." She bit her lip. "But I've known Becca and Ron for a few years now. They're good people. Kind. And very happy. I'd hate to see them get hurt. She's your mother."

"A mother I haven't seen since I was ten years old."

Ten. Devree's eyes widened. What could sweet Becca have done to turn him against her?

"Haven't you ever needed a second chance?"

He looked past her, off in the distance. "I didn't know she was here." His tone dripped sarcasm. "I didn't come here to work through my mother-inflicted emotional baggage."

"Then what did you come for? And don't tell me the job. You could get a job anywhere."

Turbulent eyes zeroed in on her. "Every memory I have of my dad is here."

"He and your mom had a good relationship?"

"According to her. But I remember them arguing a lot about living here. My mom hated it—loved Dallas."

"Really?" She frowned. "Becca loves it here now. People change, you know."

"Sometimes for the worse."

"Sometimes for the better." She hesitated. Had probably said enough. "How do you think your dad would feel about it?"

He frowned. "About what?"

"Would he want you to give your mom another chance?"

His nostrils flared.

Definitely said enough. "Just think about it." She scurried for the door, bolted for the ranch house. Away from his anger.

Two steps forward, five back where the brooding cowboy was concerned.

Something loomed just out of consciousness. It seared Brock's nose. Burnt rubber mixed with acrid sulfur. He woke to...the stench of skunk. Really close and inescapable. He threw his covers back. If only he didn't have to breathe. Was it in the barn?

Minutes later, fully dressed, he stepped out of his quarters. The cloying odor was closer to the ranch house. Great, just what guests wanted to wake up to. The reek worsened as he neared the fishing cabin.

Uptight voices sounded from the ranch house. Irate guests? Exactly what Chase and Landry didn't need. He headed that way.

"We can't possibly stay here." A snooty blonde aimed two children toward the drive.

"It'll die down by evening." Chase carried two suitcases. "You sure you don't want to stay? Spend the day in town and by the time you get back—"

"I don't think so." The woman shook her head.

"I'm sorry." An apologetic man, loaded with luggage, shrugged. "I grew up in the country, but the wife and kids, they're not used to waking up to skunk spray."

"Well, I hope you enjoyed your stay. Up until now, anyway."

"Don't worry, we'll be back."

The woman shot her husband a deadly look.

Poor guy.

Chase helped the man load the suitcases, still apologizing while the wife and children got in the car.

"It's not your fault." The man got in and drove away.

"Good news." A nasally voice came from the front porch. Devree, holding her nose. Pretty in a purple blouse and gray slacks. "The rest of the guests are staying. And your mom and dad are serving them a free breakfast for putting up with this rancid smell."

"The closer I got to the fishing cabin, the more it smelled," Brock reluctantly admitted.

Chase grimaced. "I hope it didn't have help finding its way in."

"I'll let you check it out." Devree went inside.

"Landry's upset." Chase rubbed the back of his neck. "She figures that woman will gripe to all her pretentious friends and we'll lose business."

"I think the lady failed to appreciate the charm of this place before the skunk ever sprayed. He just gave her a good excuse to get out of Dodge. I doubt she'd recommend the dude ranch to her friends, anyway."

"You're probably right."

"Go tend to Landry. I'll see if our offender is still around."

"Thanks." Chase headed inside.

Brock rushed to the fishing cabin, dug the key from his pocket. The stink was definitely worse here. The lock clicked and he opened the door, expecting to catch Pepé Le Pew in the act. But nothing seemed amiss. The smell was so potent that his eyes watered. Yet it wasn't inside. At least the striped suspect had moved on. Whoever their vandal was hadn't gotten past the new lock.

Devree had wanted to hang the final decor items today, and he still had two lighting fixtures to change out. But it would have to wait. If he couldn't stomach working here, she certainly couldn't. He'd report to Chase, see if there was anything else to do for the day. He locked up, then hurried to the ranch house.

In the lobby, Devree paced, turned to face him when the door shut behind him. "The smell is nauseating Landry, and she's upset the Dawson family left. I think Chase is taking her to an inn in town until the stink dies down."

She may be a city girl with designer clothes and a persnickety attitude to prove it, sticking her nose in where it didn't belong, but she loved her sister. So, she couldn't be all bad.

"Chase will take good care of her. Don't worry."

"You're not mad at me anymore?"

"I figure Chase needs us to work together." He gave her a pointed look. "If you don't pressure me about *her* again, we'll be fine."

"Understood." She restarted her pacing. "The skunk wasn't in the fishing cabin, was it?"

"No. But it definitely sprayed outside there. No mice, either. I think we need to start calling it honeymoon cottage A."

"Agreed. For now. Eventually, Landry and Chase will come up with cutesy names for each like the guest rooms have."

"I'm assuming the finishing touches we planned for the day are out. Anything I can do around here to ease Chase's mind?"

"I need to put up a few permanent decor items in the chapel. You can help with that, if you want."

"At your service." He tipped his hat. Though he'd hoped the skunk would have allowed him to escape her for the day. He was better off mad at her. At least that way, she couldn't reel him in. But with a truce, all bets were off as far as his heart was concerned.

"The wall decor is in my car."

He followed her out and unloaded six stacked boxes from her back seat.

"I can carry some of them."

"I'm good." He bumped the car door shut with his hip.

"The wedding party arrives in two days for the rehearsal. Do you think this smell will be gone before then?" She opened the chapel door, held it for him. "What if he has friends. Or he likes it here and decides to stick around. Is there anything we can do to keep skunks away?"

"Maybe a dog. Or a cat."

"I'll google it." She swiped the screen on her phone, then tapped in her request. "Ugh. It says dog urine deters skunks. And orange peels. Interesting."

"Maybe we should check with Chase about a dog. And he already agreed to a cat to help with the mice. Initially, I think they were getting in on their own, so a cat would encourage them to hang out somewhere else."

"He's supposed to call later once he gets Landry settled in town. I'll mention it to him." She opened one of the boxes, pulled out a chapel-window-shaped frame with decorative metal scrollwork in the center. The finish looked chipped and weathered, yet the surface was smooth.

"There are three different designs. I want two matching ones at the front, framing the stage, one on each side in the center and two in the back, framing the door."

"Just tell me which ones where."

From building luxury cabins to interior decorating. Whatever it took to help Chase. But Devree made the whole thing too pleasant. How had she gotten to him with her city-slicker ways? She was everything he'd sworn off, everything he didn't want.

As soon as Landry had the baby, Devree would be gone. Back to her beloved Dallas. He had no business getting used to having her around. Yet being near her set his heart to a different rhythm.

In the loft, Devree organized her decor items, so she could quickly whip the chapel into shape. The skunk had complicated things. They were supposed to finish the cottage today. Now, they'd be busy with it tomorrow, cutting into her wedding decor time.

Maybe she could put in some hours here after tonight's Bible study to get back on schedule. Besides, the smell wasn't as intense here as in the ranch house. Or was she getting used to it?

A loud thwack. She jumped, hurried down the ladder, scanned the expanse of green beside the chapel. Brock putting up a fence post. Right in the middle of where the outdoor reception needed to be held. Right where she planned to set up for photos for the wedding. Chase had never wanted to host weddings here, but she'd thought he was on board.

"What are you doing?" She stalked toward Brock, heels stabbing into the damp freshly sprinkled earth with each step.

He raised up, adjusted his cowboy hat. Eyes so intense she wanted to look away. "Building a fence for the petting zoo."

"No. No. No. Not right here. This is where I'll have outdoor receptions and photo sessions. I have an extremely important wedding in two days and I can't have smelly animals fouling up everything."

"I reckon you'll have to take it up with the boss man." A stubborn glint in his eyes.

At odds with the cowboy handyman. Again. "You don't understand how important this wedding is. If I ace this ceremony, it could secure my nuptial-free future."

"How's that?"

"The bride's father owns Brighton Electronics. If I impress him with a dream wedding for his daughter, he might hire me to plan his annual company retreat."

"So?"

"So. Something like that could put me on the event-planning map. And I wouldn't have to do weddings anymore. But not if Heidi the Heifer and Daisy the Donkey are stinking up everything."

Brock took off his hat, wiped his brow with the back of his gloved hand. "Chase's work order says to build it here so drive-by traffic can see it and kids will clamor to stop."

Hat head took nothing away from tall, dark and dimpled, even if he didn't get her dilemma.

"We need to postpone it. Until I can talk sense into Chase."

"So I reckon I need to pull this post up."

"Could you fill the hole too? And pack it hard enough, so no one breaks an ankle during the reception."

"Will do." He pulled the post up, threw it aside, then grabbed the shovel and went to work scooping the dirt back into the hole.

She hadn't meant to cause him extra work. But nothing and no one would stand between her and one perfect ceremony. Besides, such decisions needed to revolve around the newly constructed chapel and the dude ranch's future as a wedding venue. Even after she left.

"I'm sorry, Brock." She hoped he heard the sincerity in her tone. "Feel free to give me your best jab about women complicating everything."

"No worries. I'd rather it get built in the right place. And there's no rush. With the cottage on hold, I figured it was a good time to work on the pens. It doesn't even have to be done today."

Chase pulled his truck in the drive.

She vaulted toward him as he got out of the cab. "Is Landry all right?"

"The nausea stopped a few miles away. She's safety tucked in and sleeping at the inn with Mom."

"Why are you here?"

"I was in such a rush to get her away from the smell, I didn't pack a thing."

Devree's heart tugged. Sweet Chase—so tender, caring and totally in love with her sister. One of those rare marriages that would last.

If her sister could find lasting love, could she?

"What's going on by the chapel?"

She sucked in a deep breath, blew it out and explained the situation, careful to keep her tone unflustered.

"That can't possibly work. I thought the petting zoo was going near the goat pens."

The pressure in Devree's chest eased. "Good. I can assure you brides don't want stinky animals involved when their guests arrive."

"Valid point. Even at a dude ranch." Chase tunneled his fingers through his short hair. "I guess I was distracted."

"We'll figure it out." Brock strode toward them. "I was just gonna work on it while I had time. But I'll find something else to do."

"Actually, it's a good time. The miniature horses need a pen instead of a stall in the barn."

"If you want it seen from the road, it could go on the other side of the drive." Brock pointed to a tree-lined spot. "We could use that less dense area. Maybe take out three trees. Four, tops."

"We had an oak wilt scare year before last, thought we might lose our trees. Neither of us can stand to think of cutting them down."

"What about back a ways, so no trees need to be cut? That would still make it visible, put it a good fifty yards from the chapel and downwind."

"I don't know how the work order got so messed up. I never wanted the petting zoo anywhere near the chapel. And I never said it had to be visible from the road."

Chase frowned. "We can put a sign up for drive-by traffic. I thought it would be best if we put it near the barn."

"That's the logical location." Brock frowned. "I thought having it by the chapel was odd."

Devree had never known Chase to be that distracted. But with everything going on, she wouldn't be surprised if it hadn't been Chase at all who had filled out that work order. Had someone forged his signature?

"Sorry for the confusion, Brock." Chase blew out a heavy sigh. "I don't know what we'd have done if you hadn't shown up."

"Devree's the one who questioned it." His mouth twitched.

"Let me get some things packed, then I'll head to the barn and show you where I want it."

"Sure."

Chase strode to the ranch house.

"Poor guy." Devree hugged herself. "I've never seen him like this."

"I wish I could shoulder some of that stress for him. But I've got more bad news." He turned to face her, dug a sheet of paper from his pocket. "I don't think this is Chase's signature."

"I was thinking the same thing."

"Maybe we've been looking at this all wrong. Maybe it's you they want to sabotage."

"Me?" A chill moved over her heated skin.

"Do you have any enemies? Any ex-boyfriends with an ax to grind? Any wedding planners trying to steal your business?"

"No. Nothing like that. I dated a guy a while back, but he ended the relationship." All on his own when he'd almost married her client. "Dallas is big enough to support countless wedding planners quite well. And besides that, this was supposed to be my last wedding."

"Event planners, then? Maybe another planner doesn't want you in the field."

"I don't think so. Like I said, Dallas is big enough for all of us. I know Chase has faith in the other dude ranch owners, but I'm beginning to wonder." She vaguely remembered them being in a price war with another guest ranch when Landry had first come to Bandera. "He said others had underpriced him in the past."

"Maybe we need to check into that. Or ask around and see if any of the other ranches are struggling."

"I wish he'd call the police and let them figure this out."

"Part of me wants to keep this under our hats. Not stress him even more."

"He needs to know what's going on." And he'd be furious if he ever found out they tried to protect him by keeping things from him.

"I don't think it would hurt anything if I wait until tomorrow to tell him."

"Agreed. He's got enough on his plate today."

Brock was just as invested in Landry and Chase as she was. Softening the walls of her heart toward him.

And there was that extremely handsome thing he had going on. But that didn't mean she should let her guard down. He was still male. And she needed to run the other way.

Chapter Eight

The late afternoon sun beat down on Brock's back as he dug the last hole. Finished, he leaned on the diggers, wiped the sweat from his brow with the back of his gloved hand.

A little girl rushed his way from the ranch house with a woman lagging behind. As the child neared, he realized it was Ruby. And Scarlet.

"I can't wait for the petting zoo to open." Ruby darted right toward the hole he'd just dug.

"Easy." He grabbed her shoulders, gently stopping her in her tracks. "Watch for holes. They're as deep as you are."

Ruby looked down the hole, then up at him. "I'm not deep. I'm tall."

"I'm sorry." Scarlet stopped a few feet away. "Since Dad told her about the petting zoo, it's all she can think about."

"Well, it is exciting," he whispered conspiratorially. "I heard tell there'll be pygmy goats, sheep and miniature horses."

"Miniature horses?"

"They're about yea big, including their noggins." He held his hand less than three feet from the ground.

"Like a big dog?" Ruby's eyes grew wide.

"Exactly. Only they're horses."

"Do people ride them?"

"Kids can. And they can pull a small wagon. But they're mostly just for pets."

"When will they get here?"

"Don't tell anybody, but they're already in the barn."

Ruby whirled toward her mom. "Can we go see, Mommy?"

"We don't want to get Mr. McBride behind on his work."

"Pfft." Ruby giggled. "You mean Uncle Brock."

Scarlet's eyes grew huge. "Ruby!"

"It's okay. She broke the news the second day I was here." He was getting kind of used to the confusion in his world.

"She did? I'm so sorry."

"No worries. And as far as my work, the petting zoo isn't a priority. The cabin I was working on got skunked, so I couldn't work there today."

"Tell me about it. My client just had to pick today to see a house, so Ruby had to come to Stinky Ville after school." She pinched her nose.

"You're in real estate?"

"I am. When I have showings outside of school hours, Ruby ends up here."

"So what about seeing the mini horses?" Ruby begged.

"If you're sure you can spare the time."

"This way." He led them toward the barn.

Ruby dashed ahead.

"I'm really sorry. I shouldn't have told her who you were. I was just so excited when Dad and Becca told me you were here. I've wanted to meet you for a long time."

And he'd only learned she existed less than a week ago. "Why?"

"Becca talked about you a lot over the years." She settled her hand in the crook of his elbow, as if they were old friends. "My mom died when I was young and Becca came into our lives when I really needed her during those awkward teen years. I always wished I had a sibling, so when she told us about you, you became my fantasy brother." She let out a sheepish laugh. "It sounds silly now."

"Sorry to disappoint you."

"You haven't. I mean—I don't even know you. But I'd like to. Have you thought about that dinner I mentioned?"

"I'll have to check my schedule."

"Look, I know this whole step-kin thing is a lot for you to digest. But Becca has been such a blessing in our lives. Such a wonderful influence on me and my daughter. Drew's mom died a few years into our marriage. So if not for Becca, Ruby wouldn't have a grandma."

The sincerity in her tone tugged at him.

"I'll think about it." If Mom told them the truth. He couldn't stomach sitting through a family gathering and tiptoeing around the secrets of his childhood.

"Fair enough." Scarlet looked toward the barn. "Wait up, Ruby. Don't you dare open any of the pens."

"I won't, Mommy. But hurry."

They reached the barn and stepped inside the wide galley between the stalls.

"They're over here." He led the way to the fourth stall where Sweetpea and Peanut were munching on hay, then helped Ruby climb up on the slatted wood gate so she could see.

The pint-size sisters looked up from beneath their pouf of bang-like manes resting across their foreheads. With pale golden coats and wooly cream-colored manes and tails, they were maybe two and half feet tall.

"They're so cute." Ruby's gaze fastened on the duo.

"Adorable." Scarlet leaned her elbows on the railing.

"Thanks for letting us see. Come on, Ruby. Brock needs to get back to work."

"But I want to pet them."

"You'll get to another time. We need to get supper before Bible study tonight." She helped Ruby down, then turned to Brock. "Think about that supper. The invitation's open whenever you're ready."

"Thanks." He watched them go.

As far as stepsisters went, Scarlet wouldn't be a bad one. But his mom was another story. How could the same woman abandon her child, then end up being a great mom to someone else's teenager?

Sleeping with a dust mask on last night hadn't been fun for Devree, but at least the skunk smell was waning this morning. Landry and Chase were home and the guests were happy. The petting zoo was well underway and not anywhere near the chapel. It was late afternoon and honeymoon cottage A was almost complete.

Brock hung a shelf made from plantation shutters. "How's that?"

"Perfect. That's it. Can I help you with anything?"

"I just have the final chandelier in the bedroom to hang."

"I can hold tools or the flashlight for you."

"If you don't mind. And don't have anything else to do."

"After all the curtain rods and pictures you've hung for me, it's the least I can do." She headed to the bedroom with his booted footfalls behind her.

Brock handed her a flashlight, fiddled in the breaker box and the room went dark.

It took her eyes a minute to adjust as she moved to the curtain, tucked it in the tieback. The huge live oak outside the window shaded the area but allowed some sunlight in.

"Is it okay if we stand on the bed?" He sat on the king-size mattress and pulled one boot off, then the other.

"Sure." She sat beside him, kicked off her heels, then pulled her feet up.

He stood, offered his hand, helped her up.

This felt too close in the darkened room. She took a step back.

"The chandelier and tools are on the nightstand."

"Just tell me what you need me to do."

"I must say, I like this fixture." He dug a screwdriver out of his pocket, went to work loosening the cover plate on the antler chandelier with her shining the flashlight for him.

"I compromised on the curtains. And this one will go in Chase's office at the new house."

The cover plate came loose and Brock touched his rubber-handled pliers to the wires. Nothing. Next, he cut the wire in two and handed her the chandelier. "Got it?"

"Yep." She carried it to the empty nightstand, a bit wobbly, walking on a mattress with the heavy fixture. But then she stepped too close to the edge, and almost lost her balance. "Whoa."

Strong arms came around her waist from behind. "Easy."

Goodness, he smelled good. And felt good. Muscled and sturdy. Protective.

"You okay?"

Not really. But all she did was nod.

His arms slipped away and he took the fixture from her. "Sorry about that. It is heavy."

He set it down on the nightstand, then walked across the width of the bed and picked up the new chandelier.

She forced herself to concentrate on the light fixture. Weathered white metal with blue mason jars surrounding each teardrop-shaped bulb and matching crystals under-neath each light. The perfect accent for the room.

But she'd rather concentrate on the cowboy.

"Can you hold this one while I attach the wire? It's not as heavy." As she took it from him, their fingers grazed and her breath caught. Thankfully, he didn't seem to notice and went to work on the wiring as he held the flashlight.

Several turns with his pliers later, he dug orange con-nectors from his pocket and screwed them into place, then wrapped black tape around the wiring. He fished several screws and a driver from his pocket and reached for the chandelier.

She handed it to him, managing not to touch him this time.

He attached the cover plate and let the fixture hang, then helped her down and went to the switch box. Light flooded the room. "How's that?"

"Perfect."

"I believe honeymoon cottage A is ready for the happy couple."

"What a relief. Now just some fresh towels and we're set. Which reminds me, I meant to put the clean towels I brought over in the dryer." She hurried to the living room, grabbed the laundry basket full of wet terrycloth.

"Let me get that." His hands closed over hers and he whisked the basket away, leaving her struggling for air as she followed him to the utility closet by the bathroom.

He opened the dryer, dumped the towels in and started it.

"I meant to have them drying while I worked, then fold them before I left. Guess I'll come back later." She headed for the front door, eager to lose him. So she could breathe right. "Since the cabin is finished and it's Thurs-day, I'll be busy decorating the wedding chapel the rest of the day and preparing for the wedding party's arrival and rehearsal tomorrow."

"And I'll be busy finishing up Chase and Landry's house."

So they probably wouldn't see each other much until next week. Why did that bother her?

"Do you smell that?"

She sniffed the air. A hint of something...unpleasant. "What is it?"

"Dead animal."

"Oh, no. You didn't put any rat poison out, did you?"

"No." He walked around the room, sniffing, then down the hall, stopping at the dryer. "It's coming from here." He opened the door, interrupting the tumbling towels.

The odor permeated the room. She pinched her nose between finger and thumb. "Oh, that's worse than the skunk. Is it the towels?"

"No. It's under the cabin. Probably coming up through the dryer vent. We may have found Pepé Le Pew."

"Oh, no."

"Relax. It's a good thing. If we get rid of him, he won't smell anymore. And the wedding is still two days away. I'll crawl under and see what I can find, but you'll probably have to rewash those towels."

"Want me to hold the light?" Though she really didn't want to. She longed to run to the ranch house where the air was breathable.

He chuckled. "You go on. This will get dirty. I'll set up a floodlight."

"Thank you. Thank you. Thank you." She laughed.

But why was walking away from him so hard? Even with a dead skunk in the mix.

The crawl space was wide open. Only human hands could unlatch it. Why hadn't he thought to check it before now? Brock shone his light under the cabin. Not his idea of fun—crawling in tight spaces where rattlesnakes might hole up to get away from the heat.

He hurried to the tool shed, grabbed a floodlight and thick work gloves, then returned to the cabin. With the floodlight set up just inside the crawl space, he could see the dryer vent, then scanned the area for any slithering reptiles. Nothing seemed amiss. He lay down on his belly, wiggled his shoulders through the opening and dragged himself along on his elbows, shining the flashlight in front of him.

A good fifteen feet later, he made it to the dryer vent, shone his light around. The stench was horrendous, but no body. Could it be in the vent? He touched the silver accordion tubing. Heavy, like there was something in it. He took in a deep breath, held it, and reached into the vent, grabbed whatever it was by the tail and tugged.

Pepé Le Pew was in his hand. Dead and stinky. He gagged, sucked in another breath, turned and crawled back to the opening fast. Less concerned about snakes with the stench flooding his airways. Near the hole, he threw the skunk out, then crawled out like a drowning man.

Outside, he grabbed the dead animal, obviously roadkill, bolted for the woods and threw it as far as he could. Well out of range of any guests.

"Not in my job description." He jerked the gloves off, dumped them in a trash bag and tied it up. With the air fresher, he retrieved the floodlight, latched the crawlspace and headed for his quarters. Never had he wanted a shower so badly.

Movement on the back porch of the ranch house drew his attention. Devree swaying on the swing, her hand clamped over her mouth, as if she were trying not to laugh.

"You thought that was funny?"

"I'm sorry. I've never seen you move so fast."

"Glad you enjoyed the show. But we have a problem."

She sobered. "What?"

"The crawl space was open. Someone opened it."

"You think someone planted the skunk? You mean, like saw it and shooed it under the cabin."

"No, I think they saw it freshly dead on the road or maybe even hit it with their vehicle, then brought it here and shoved it in the dryer vent. So it would stink up the only honeymoon cottage we have ready on the week of your big wedding."

"That sounds pretty desperate." Maybe even unhinged. "But the skunk ran off guests. I still think that's what the guilty party wants." She tapped a finger against her chin. "But they may have gone too far this time. Whoever it is should be wearing the evidence. We initially smelled skunk. Whoever put it under there couldn't have gotten away unscathed."

"Exactly. Fill Chase in while I shower. We'll start with ranch employees, then move on to the other dude ranches in the area. Find out if anyone has been skunked lately."

"Without letting Landry know what's going on." Worry dwelled in the depths of her blue eyes.

"Of course. I think it's time to fill him in on the forged signature too." He jogged toward his quarters. Whoever was doing this was stooping to an all-time low. Attacking a pregnant lady's business. And not just any pregnant lady. His friend's wife. And Devree's sister. Whatever it took, he'd find the culprit and remove that worry from her eyes.

"Who would pull this?" Chase stalked toward the barn.

"Maybe we'll know soon." Devree had to practically run to keep up with him and Brock.

"You should have stayed at the house," he barked over his shoulder. "This might get ugly."

"I have a right to know who's trying to disrupt my sister's life."

They made it to the barn and the foreman met them under the shade of a live oak. "What's going on?"

"This may sound like a strange question, Troy." Chase adjusted his cowboy hat. "But have any of the hands smelled like skunk lately?"

"Not that I've noticed. What's this about?"

"We've had some vandalism lately. I know it sounds crazy." Chase filled him in on the mice, the rooster, the cows, the forged signature and the skunk. "We're just trying to figure out who."

"I'm sorry for the trouble and the lost guests, but I can't imagine any of my crew pulling such shenanigans. They're all hard workers. I'd vouch for every one of them."

"Has anybody called in sick in the last few days?" Brock shifted his weight from one foot to the other.

"Lee Jackson. He was out today and yesterday with that upper respiratory crud that's been going around. Sounded horrible on the phone. You don't think it's him? He's a go-getter and he's never missed a day's work before."

"We're just trying to get to the bottom of this." Devree tried to soften it. "And please don't tell Landry any of it. We have to shield her from the stress."

"Of course not. I'm praying for the baby and the missus."

Chase squeezed Troy's shoulder. "Thanks. It means a lot."

"I did hear something strange today though."

"What's that?"

"One of the hands was at a bar in town last weekend.

He said Wilson Carter was in there bragging about how some guy paid him to quit his job here."

"That is strange." Chase frowned. "Let me know if you hear anything else."

"Will do, boss."

Chase headed back to the house. "If I get Lee's address, can you drive over with me and see if his place smells like skunk?"

"Yes," Devree and Brock answered in unison as they followed Chase.

"Not you." Chase stopped long enough to point a finger at her. "You stay out of this. I shouldn't have let you go to the barn. The vandal may have heard us and try something stupid. I've already got one woman to protect, and I don't need two."

"I'll go." Brock met her gaze. "Without you."

She stared him down, but he didn't give an inch. They climbed the steps of the ranch-house porch. "Who's Wilson Carter?" Brock asked.

"Our old handyman." Paid to leave Chase in the lurch. This definitely wasn't about her. She stopped as the two men went inside. They didn't seem to notice, and she bolted for Brock's truck.

Thankfully, it wasn't locked and she climbed in the back seat, hunkered down. The cab was hot as an oven.

Minutes later, the crunch of footsteps on gravel. Both front doors of the cab opened and she held her breath as the men climbed in.

"Where did Devree go?" Chase asked.

"I didn't see her. Maybe she went to the chapel to decorate some more for the wedding tomorrow."

"I should have told Dad to keep an eye on her too. I figured I'd have to physically block her from getting in the truck with us. She's too stubborn for her own good."

"She loves her sister to a fault though. When it comes down to it, you can't condemn her for that."

"I guess not."

She grinned. Several miles down the road, she raised up. "Hey, guys."

Brock's eyes widened, met hers in the rearview mirror. "Don't you have a wedding chapel to decorate?"

"Should have known. Turn the truck around, Brock," Chase growled.

"There's no time," she insisted. "Lee Jackson might be washing his truck down in tomato juice as we speak."

Brock's eyes narrowed.

She didn't flinch.

"You're not going. Turn around right here." Chase pointed out a wide driveway.

Brock slowed the truck.

She closed her eyes. "Think about it, Chase. What if it's not Lee? Maybe our thug was lurking in the barn listening. If I go with you, I'll be safe."

A sigh huffed out of him and Brock sped up again.

She should be decorating the chapel. But there was no way she'd be able to focus while some lunatic tried to put her sister out of business.

Chapter Nine

Brock had a bad feeling about this. They should have taken Devree back.

"According to the mailboxes, it should be the next drive on the right." She pointed up ahead.

"You stay in the truck," Chase ordered.

"I have a really good nose."

"In the truck, I said."

"Maybe I'll just roll down the windows."

Brock slowed, saw the house number on the box, and turned in. A white pickup in the drive. As he opened the door, a whiff of skunk assailed him.

"Smell that?" Devree announced from the back seat. "I think we've got him."

"And you're staying here."

"What about calling the police?"

"No. He's just a kid. I'm gonna try to figure out his angle and fire him. Maybe he just needs another chance."

"You're a good guy, Chase. For all your bluster, deep down, you're a softy."

"Grrr," he growled. "Don't tell anybody. Either one of you."

Brock and Chase got out of the truck. As they neared

the farmhouse, Brock looked back a few times, expecting to see Devree. He was anticipating having to physically pick her up and stuff her back in the cab, then one of them sticking around to babysit her in order to make her stay put.

But she didn't get out. Maybe for all her bluster, this confrontation frightened her. Or she respected her brother-in-law enough not to cause him further stress. Either way, he was glad she'd surrendered.

Chase knocked on the door.

"I'm sick," hollered a voice from inside, followed by a round of coughing.

"It's Chase Donovan. I need to talk to you."

"I'm contagious."

"Come outside."

"I don't want you to get sick."

Chase turned the door knob. Unlocked. "Come out or I'm coming in."

"Okay, okay." The floor creaked from inside. The door opened a crack. A young cowboy, barely twenty, turned away and went into a fit of coughing.

Sounded fake. They waited for it to end.

"I smell skunk." Chase glared at the kid.

The kid's face went red. "I hit one with my truck on the way home from the doctor today."

"Or was that Tuesday night and you brought it back to the ranch and stuck it in the dryer vent of the old fishing cabin to go along with the mouse infestation you caused. You also cut the fence so Rusty got out, along with the hole in the cows' fence, and forged my signature on the work order for the petting zoo."

"I—I—I," the kid stammered. "I don't know what you're talking about."

"I think you do." Chase didn't back down. He looked as if he might tear into the kid.

"Okay, you're right. I did all those things. Are you gonna call the cops?"

"If you tell me why you vandalized my ranch, I might give you another chance."

"Nash Porter is my uncle." The kid swallowed hard. "He couldn't pay his bills, got drunk and ended up in jail. All because of you."

Chase's jaw clenched. "I fired him because he made the women at the ranch uncomfortable, he was disrespectful and insubordinate. You're fired too. I better not see you around my place again, and if I hear of you getting in any more trouble, I'll call the police. Are we clear?"

"Yes, sir."

"We'll mail your final check." Chase turned away.

"You're getting a second chance." Brock told the kid. "Use it for good and don't end up like your uncle."

"Yes, sir."

Brock followed Chase to his truck, opened the door.

"What happened?" Devree asked from the back seat.

"He admitted everything." Brock met her gaze in the rearview mirror as he started the engine, backed out of the drive.

"Why?"

"His uncle is the troublemaker I told you about. I didn't know they were related." Chase sighed. "Lee blamed me for his uncle ending up in jail."

"What about Wilson Carter? Did Lee's uncle pay him off?"

"I doubt it since he couldn't pay his bills."

"Why don't we go ask Wilson who paid him? He lives around here, right?"

"I'm sure part of his job was to keep quiet about it. He probably doesn't even remember spouting off in the bar."

"Did you call the police? Sounds like Lee's on the same track as his uncle."

"No. I gave him a chance to turn it around."

"I sure hope he takes advantage of it."

"Me too."

"Well, at least we got to the bottom of it." Brock turned onto the highway. "Maybe things will settle down now."

"Once Landry has the baby, I'll tell her about all this and how you gave that boy a second chance." Devree patted Chase's shoulder.

"You'll ruin my reputation."

"You're gonna be a great dad."

Her gaze met Brock's in the mirror. Mutual respect for Chase passing between them without words. Maybe they did have something in common.

Devree was cutting it close with her wedding party arriving today and the rehearsal tonight. She wound tulle around the pillars on each side of the stage, draping it just so. She'd done it so many times, she could almost do it in her sleep. Next, the ivy-and-pearl garland.

The door to the chapel opened. "Heard you could use a hand." Brock strode up the aisle.

"I thought you were busy with Chase and Landry's house."

"I did too. But Landry doesn't want you climbing the ladder in here alone."

"Well, you're too late, I've already been up there and I'm none the worse for wear. She's a worrier, but I'm fine." Finished with the pillars, she started to move the ladder to the lattice archway behind where the preacher would stand.

His hands landed on hers. "I'll get that."

Warmth moved up her arms. Reluctantly, she pulled away. "Over here, then. Underneath the archway."

He placed the ladder for her as she grabbed more tulle from a plastic bin and started up the rungs.

"I can do the climbing if you'll tell me what to do."

"I'm fine. And you don't seem like a decorating guru."

"I'll take that as a compliment. Guess I'll stand here and make sure you don't fall, then."

She climbed the ladder, wound the tulle through the lattice. "Can you hand me the ivy-and-pearl garland."

"This?" He held up the greenery.

She took it from him, wound it among the tulle, then started down the ladder to do the sides. But her foot slipped. "Oh!" She teetered, lost her balance. Strong arms caught her, lowered her safely to her feet but didn't let go.

"What are you thinking climbing a ladder barefoot?"

"It was either that or my heels."

"Why do you always wear those ridiculous stilts?"

"The wedding party is arriving today. I wanted to look the part."

His gaze held hers prisoner, then lowered to her mouth as he dipped his head.

Her breath hitched as his lips neared hers.

The chapel door opened and they sprang apart.

"Devree. It's lovely." Millicent Brighton stepped inside. "Miranda will be so happy."

"Thanks for putting so much into our little girl's special day." Phillip Brighton followed her as they continued down the aisle.

"Every bride should have the perfect wedding. This is Brock McBride." She managed to keep her voice steady. "He's the handyman here. My sister was worried about me being on the ladder, so she sent Brock to help. I'm finished with the high stuff now, if you need to go."

"If you do any more ladder climbing, call me."

"I will."

He turned away, strolled down the aisle and out the door.

As the bride's parents chattered on about the quaint chapel, the decorations and the wedding, one thought crowded everything else out.

Brock had almost kissed her.

And even more than that—she'd wanted him to.

The wedding rehearsal and dinner kept Devree busy for the rest of the day and evening. Brock hadn't seen her since he'd almost tested the sweetness of her lips. Something he hadn't planned on. Not at all. The attraction between them was getting out of hand.

Yet, it was more than attraction. She was empathetic, loyal and family meant everything to her. The kind of woman who, once she committed her heart to someone, wouldn't leave. The kind of woman he'd looked for his whole adult life. But, there was the Dallas-thing. And that created a big hurdle.

He tucked the kennel under his arm, grabbed the bag of food and supplies, then hurried to the cabin. The light was on inside. *Huh?* He hesitated. Maybe the bride and groom? No, the bride had a room in the ranch house and the groom was in one of the hunting cabins. They weren't scheduled to be here until after the ceremony tomorrow night.

Had Lee Jackson come back to cause more trouble? Brock set his load down, opened the door, ready for battle.

Devree whirled around, her mouth open, obviously ready to scream. Instead, she clamped a hand to her heart. "What are you doing here?"

"I could ask the same thing?"

"Making sure there are no stray mice."

"I told you I didn't want you coming here alone."

"Lee Jackson doesn't work here anymore."

"But he might be mad he got fired and he doesn't live far enough away for my comfort. And don't forget, someone is willing to pay people to disrupt things around here."

"But we're onto them both. Surely they won't pull anything else. So why are you here?"

"Same as you."

A meow sounded from the porch.

"What was that?"

"My solution. Come on, I'll show you." He stepped out, waited for her to follow, then opened the kennel. The orange-and-white cat tumbled out. He filled the bowl with food as the cat checked out his new territory.

"He's so cute."

"I got him from the lady at the coffee shop. She said he's a great mouser. There are two more in the barn."

"Will they stay here?" Devree squatted, reached her hand palm up toward the cat, but he ignored her, rubbed against Brock's leg and then went to the food bowl.

"He'll warm up to you. The barn will be safe and they'll stick around as long as we feed them and there aren't any dogs to pester them."

"But Chase is considering getting a dog."

"We'll find one that doesn't mind cats."

The cat finished eating, slinked over and rubbed against Devree's leg. She stooped and he let her pick him up. "Oh, you're just a little sweetie." She rubbed her cheek against the cat, scratched his jaw until he purred. "I've always wanted a cat, but Mom is allergic, and my apartment doesn't allow pets."

"I think he likes you and wants to be yours."

"But I'm not staying here. And I wouldn't be able to take him home when I leave."

She still thought of Dallas as home. How could he even

think about getting involved with her? But as she set the cat down, he was drawn to her once more.

"Maybe Morris can be my cat while I'm here. And after I leave, he can be yours."

"I'm not planning on staying, either." Especially, if she didn't. "But I guess that'll work. For now. Why Morris?"

"Remember those old cat food commercials with the orange cat?"

He did. But she intrigued him more. Intent on finishing what he'd started yesterday, he stepped close. "I was hoping you might decide to stay. I mean—Landry will need you even after the baby comes."

Her gaze locked on his. "Is that the only reason?"

"No." He dipped his head and she stood on tiptoe as he slipped his arms around her waist. Their lips met, soft and sweet as her hands inched up his shoulders.

But she stiffened, pulled away. "We can't do this. I'm only here to relieve my sister's stress and ace a wedding. I have a business to revamp back in Dallas. A relationship with you won't fit into the plan."

"I'm sorry." Regret spread warm and heavy in his chest. "I shouldn't have done that and it won't happen again." His arms dropped to his sides and he walked away. He didn't stop until he slipped inside his quarters.

What had he been thinking? He hadn't. She was intent on leaving him behind for her beloved city, just like his mother had.

Chapter Ten

The wedding rehearsal and dinner had gone off without a hitch last night. Now, if the ceremony would just come together glitch-free, maybe Devree would be on her way to planning Brighton Electronics' company retreat. She lay in bed a few minutes longer, reveling in the rooster-less morning, reliving Brock's kiss despite her need to forget it.

Hoofbeats nearby and cattle bawling interrupted the peaceful moment. What was going on down there? She got up, went to the window and peered out. Hooping cowboys on horseback herding cows. A cattle drive? On the very day of her most important wedding ever.

Five minutes later, she was dressed and dashing down the stairs, out the door. Troy, the foreman, made a loop around a stray cow, got it back in line.

"Troy!" she cupped her hands around her mouth to be heard.

"Morning, Miss Devree." He tipped his hat.

"What's going on here?"

"A cattle drive."

"But I have a wedding today." Her tone was on the verge of panic. "The cattle drives aren't supposed to happen on the same weekends as weddings."

"Apparently, Lee set it up before he left and got our guests all excited about it."

She looked past him. Three city slickers having the time of their lives. "You have to cancel it."

"What's going on?" Brock asked behind her.

"We can't have a cattle drive the day of the wedding." She was near tears and seeing him after last night didn't help her nerves.

"Can you move the cattle to the back of the property?" Brock shouted.

"Sure." Troy called orders to his hands. Within minutes, the herd was headed away from the ranch. Dust swirled in their wake, then began to settle.

"Problem solved." Brock's posture was stiff as he strode away.

Except the problem stirring in her heart.

She hurried inside to apologize and calm the bride. In the foyer, the father-of-the-bride—the man she really needed to impress, descended the stairs. A grim frown on his face.

"I'm so sorry, Mr. Brighton. We had a scheduling issue, but they've moved the cattle drive to the back pasture and you won't even know it's going on."

He opened his mouth.

"Daddy, wasn't that fun?" Miranda hurried down the steps, slid her arm into the crook of her father's elbow. "I've never seen a real cattle drive before. What a great way to begin my wedding day."

"I'm glad you enjoyed it." Apparently her bride wasn't as metropolitan as she'd thought. "Maybe you can come back sometime and go on a drive."

Miranda laughed. "I don't want to get that close. But I just had the best idea. Maybe Daddy could have the company retreat here. And the men could go on a cattle drive."

Great idea. "The dude ranch is open for events and I'd be happy to plan it for you, if you decide to go that route." Devree smiled, as if she hadn't been conspiring since she'd agreed to plan the wedding.

"Something to think on. But right now, I'd like to take my daughter to breakfast while she still has my last name."

"Of course. Just let me know if you need anything."

They strolled across to the dining room. As the doors closed behind them, Devree pumped her fist in a victory gesture.

The front door opened and Brock stepped inside. "Guess everything's good in here." He barely looked at her.

She told him about her conversation with the bride's father. "That's what this whole wedding has been about for me."

"I'm glad you're getting what you want." He strode toward the dining room.

Except, she wasn't. Deep down—she wanted him in her life. But he'd never move to Dallas and she could never stay here. How had she let herself get so attached to him?

From the porch of the ranch house, Brock watched the newlyweds flee the chapel as guests threw birdseed and stopped them for last-minute hugs. Reception over, the couple climbed into the waiting horse-drawn carriage and were whisked away to the cottage. The crowd dispersed to their cars. Once he saw the parents of the bride leave, he stood and headed that way. Though he'd rather do anything else. But he couldn't turn down a pregnant lady's request.

Inside the chapel, Devree was already on the ladder, unwinding poufy white netting from the pillars. Barefoot.

She stopped, turned to see who'd come in. "What are you doing here?"

"Landry sent me to help you clean up."

"Surely, wedding cleanup isn't in your job description."

"Neither is digging a skunk out of a dryer vent. But I'll do whatever Chase and Landry need for as long as I'm here."

"Suit yourself." She shrugged. "I'll go move my trailer around front, so we can load this stuff up."

"You have your own trailer?"

"It's small, but all this stuff is mine. I need somewhere to store it and it makes it easy to transport with a trailer."

"Why have I not seen it?"

"It's in the garage at the new house." She grabbed her purse, slipped on her shoes. "Be right back."

The one place he hadn't been on the property. "What can I do while you're gone?"

"Move the pillars and those totes I've already packed on the front pew to the door."

Left alone, he moved the items she'd requested. None of them were heavy, but they were bulky and awkward. Just as he moved the last tub, she stepped back inside.

"Want me to take these on out?"

"No. The arbor needs to go in first, then the pillars, then the totes." She started to move the ladder.

"I've got it." He manhandled it from her, grazing her hands along the way, stirring his pulse. "Where do you want it?"

"Under the arbor so I can take the ivy and tulle off."

He moved the ladder. "Do you use the greenery and netting for every wedding?"

"Most of them. Sometimes a bride will get picky and want something else."

"Why don't you just leave it on until you get a picky bride?"

"It doesn't keep as well. It gets dingy and frayed and I don't always use the same fabric. Besides, it doesn't take long to put it on or take it off. I've done it so many times, I could do it with my eyes closed if I had to." She loosened the last bit of netting and stepped down from the ladder. But didn't stumble this time. The air crackled between them as her gaze caught his.

He stepped aside as she unwound the decorations from one side of the archway and he tackled the other. He moved underneath the arbor, now stripped free of trappings, and lifted it. "This thing's heavy."

"I didn't mean for you to do it alone." She grabbed one side. "Let me help."

"I've got it. Just get the door."

She let go and hurried for the exit, held it open for him, then unlocked the trailer and stood out of the way as he walked his load inside.

"How do you handle this stuff on your own?"

"I don't. I have a guy."

Of course, she did. His breath caught. If she was involved with someone else, what was she doing kissing him? Technically, he'd kissed her, but she'd definitely kissed him back.

"His mother is a florist I use often. He's sixteen and a fullback on his football team. I hire him to do my heavy lifting."

Oh. That kind of guy. "So what's on your agenda, now that the wedding is over?"

"I'll be decorating the new honeymoon cottages. And I'll help get the new house move-in ready for Chase and Landry. They approved my contest idea, so I'll be doing publicity for that along with finding vendors to volunteer services for the winning retreat. What's next for you?"

"Getting Chase and Landry moved into the new house, fixing whatever needs fixing around here and helping with the new cabins." Which meant, they'd still be working together much of the time. With this attraction sizzling between them. But it was more than that. She'd gotten past all his defenses. Yet Dallas was too big of a gulf for them to span.

"So when can they move?"

"Technically—Friday. Once the painters finish, we'll do the flooring and finish work. The furniture is arriving Thursday, so everything will be ready. But Chase wants to wait until the next week to make certain the paint fumes are gone."

"He won't take any chances with the baby." The corners of her mouth kicked up, a dreamy expression softened her eyes. "Not many men like him in the world. And I'm so glad Landry found him after everything she went through before."

"Yet their happiness—even after losing their first child—hasn't restored your faith in love?"

"Most of the time, it doesn't work out so well." She rolled her eyes, slipped her shoes off, hurried back up the ladder.

Silly woman. Must she wear those excuses for shoes even when cleaning up after the wedding?

But deep down, he hoped she'd lose her balance again. So he could catch her.

No Devree at morning service. They must be on a different schedule now. The closing prayer ended with an echo of amens. Brock shot from his seat, headed for the door. Ron or his mom wouldn't get the chance to pull him aside today. He was out of here.

"Hello, I'm Ella Jones." A salt-and-pepper-haired woman headed him off. "I'm on housekeeping detail here at the dude ranch."

"Brock McBride." At least his last name wouldn't tip

her off since it was different than his mom's. "Handyman." He clasped her outstretched hand.

"Oh, yes. I heard they hired someone. Do you sing, young man?"

"I'm afraid not."

"I'm trying to put a choir together. Do you know of anyone employed here who does?"

"Brock has a wonderful voice," his mom said appearing on his left.

"Really? Are you trying to hold out on me, Mr. McBride?"

"Not at all. She hasn't heard me sing since I was a child." He spared her a glance.

Color suffused her face. "That's true. But he had a wonderful voice the last time I heard him at ten years old. Usually if a person can sing as a child, they don't lose the ability as an adult."

"That's true. You knew Becca when you were little?"

"It was a long time ago." Brock worked at keeping his tone pleasant for Ella's sake.

"Listen, the chapel is mainly for dude ranch employees and guests." Ella looped her arm through the crook of his elbow, leaned close as if they were conspiring. "It'll be difficult since we attend on separate shifts. But all congregations need a choir. How can I convince you to join?"

"Let me try." Mom smiled up at him. "Since we go way back."

"Excellent idea." Ella patted his shoulder. "I'll be expecting you in the choir, Mr. McBride. Nice meeting you." She moved on, leaving them alone.

Brock looked around. They were alone. Even Ron was gone. As if the entire congregation had conspired to get them together.

"I'll pretend you tried to talk me into it." He started past her.

But she touched his arm. "Ella's watching and if you go scowling off, she'll ask questions. Besides, I never got the chance to ask you how you like the ranch?"

"It's all right." Except she was here. He pulled away from her.

Her hand dropped to her side. "You've relieved a lot of Chase's stress."

"That's why I'm sticking around." Not to reunite with her.

"What's next on your to-do list?"

"Get Chase and Landry moved into the new house. Finishing touches and paint. Trim work and flooring." *Get through Dad's birthday on Tuesday.* Did she even remember the significance of the date? "Setting up the nursery and furniture."

"My crew is all set to clean. Just let me know when."

He'd be sure to make himself scarce, then. "Your crew?"

"I'm head of housekeeping."

If the Donovans knew the truth, would they trust her with that position?

"Look, why don't you come to the house for lunch? Ron would love to visit with you. And I would too."

He wanted to bite her head off. Tell her all the reasons he'd never step foot in her house. But standing inside a church wasn't the proper place and the manners Mama Simons had instilled in him came to the surface. "No, thank you."

"Because I haven't told Ron everything?"

"The subject will come up. Where was I as a kid? What did Dad's family supposedly tell me to turn me against you? I won't go through that."

"I just want to spend time with you."

"Then tell him the truth," Brock growled.

"He's such a good man." Mom's eyes begged for mercy. "I don't want to lose him."

"If he's the kind of man who'll leave over past mistakes, maybe he's not worth having."

"It's not that. Ron is a stickler for the truth. He'll be deeply hurt that I withheld my past from him."

"Maybe you should have thought of that before you married him. Until then, I think we've said all we need to say."

Eyes glossy, she nodded her head as if she'd expected him to decline. "Will you at least consider singing in the choir? God wants us to use the talents He's given us."

"God expects us to keep our word when we say we'll leave someone alone too." His jaw clenched.

"Grandma." Ruby ran up and hugged his mom. "Grandpa said the petting zoo is set up. When can I come, Uncle Brock?" She lowered her voice to a whisper on the last bit.

"Let me know next time you're at the ranch after school and I'll give you a private tour."

"I can't wait." She looked up at his mom. "Is Uncle Brock coming to lunch with us?"

"Sorry. Not today, kiddo." He twirled her curly ponytail around his finger, then strode away. Actually, never—if Grandma was invited too.

Who was his mom to tell him what God wanted? God wanted parents to stay off drugs. To remember where they left their children. To pick them up from the babysitter. To love them. Not to abandon them. To do everything opposite of what she'd done.

The chatter and song of various birds serenaded the morning sun as Brock stepped out on his porch. His cell rang. He swiped his hand down his work shirt and dug in his pocket. The contractor. "Brock here. What can I do for you?"

"Can you retrieve the redhead?"

"You mean Devree? What's she doing?"

"She's here at the new house, second-guessing everything we do. Can you call her off?"

"I can't promise anything." He tucked his phone back in his pocket, jumped in his truck and headed that way. Minutes later, he killed his engine. No power tools sounded. Had she managed to single-handedly bring construction to a standstill?

The buzz of a compressor started up, followed by the thunk of a nail gun, along with the whine of a circular saw echoing from inside. Okay, maybe not even Devree Malone could stop progress.

He opened the door, stepped inside. There was sawdust everywhere. A thick fog hung in the air, what with the doorways to the rest of the house closed off with heavy plastic sheeting. Exposed insulation and multi-colored slats of wood lined the walls.

Devree's mouth was moving, but the compressor drowned her out. "Excuse me!"

The compressor silenced just as she shouted. All eyes turned on her.

"Ahem." Her face turned four shades of red. "As I said, I'm Devree Malone—I'll be overseeing interior design. Is there any way y'all could do the sawing outside, so there's not dust everywhere?"

Snickers.

The gray-haired construction foreman, Ben Myers, stepped toward her. "Like I said, sawing inside saves time and we're on a tight schedule here."

"But cleaning up all this sawdust will take time."

"Not as much time as carrying our lumber in and out.

It's a construction site. Things get messy. But we'll clean up when we're done." He propped his hands on his tool belt. "Anything else?"

Not easily intimidated, she straightened her spine, raised her chin. "The lumber is all willy-nilly, mismatched with no pattern."

"That's the way it's supposed to be, according to the work order. It's a focal point." The compressor started up again. Ben held his hands palm up, then turned away and went back to work with his men.

She scanned the walls once more, dug her phone from her pocket, took pictures from different angles as the sawdust swirled. Noticing him, she turned to give him a mouthful, only he couldn't hear a thing she said.

He grabbed her elbow, pointed her toward the exit. Thankfully, she complied. Outside, the noise faded as he shut the door behind them.

"If I'm going to oversee the design, you have to make them listen to me."

"He's right on the sawing. It would be time-consuming to do it outside. And they need to get the wall done, so the painters can tackle the rest of the room. I told the contractor I'd help with the finish work after that to speed things along."

"Let me know when I can set up the nursery. I want to do that for Landry."

"Will Wednesday work?"

"Perfect. But do you really think the house will be dust-free enough by then?"

"I've seen thousands of construction sites. Trust me, when it's over, you won't know there was ever sawdust involved." Especially with his mom on the job. They might have their issues, but she excelled when it came to cleaning.

"I thought that wall was all supposed to be barn wood."

She scrolled on her tablet, turned it to show him. A picture of a reclaimed lumber wall with little variety in color.

"Barn wood is usually all different colors from sun and weather. As long as they're putting it on the right wall, I don't see a problem."

"But there has to be some sort of pattern."

"Huh?"

All animated, she drew in the air with her hands. "A pattern—light, dark, medium."

"You mean like stripes?"

"Something. Right now, it's a mismatched mess."

"Can I see your tablet?"

Her right eyebrow lifted, but she handed him the tablet and he googled *rustic wood interior*. Several walls popped up with a mix of wood shades. She stepped beside him to see. Apple shampoo tickled his senses.

"See, it's a new trend." He tried to ignore her nearness, her cinnamon hair against his arm. "You blend different shades. There's no pattern and it turns out great."

"If you say so." Her nose crinkled. "It seems like the wood should at least go from wall to wall. With them layering it in short pieces, it looks like a mess. Apparently, the mix of shades couldn't be helped. But shouldn't there be some sort of order instead of chaos?"

"You're not into rustic design, huh?"

"Not really. Rustic weddings are always a challenge for me."

"Then I reckon you'll just have to trust me. I'll admit it looks like a mess right now, but wait until you see the big picture."

Her blue eyes met his. And he had to fight the pull he felt toward her. She'd made her intentions about her future clear. "If I send the pictures to Chase, he probably wouldn't see the problem. Should I bother Landry with it? Would it stress her out?"

"From what I understood, Landry made the call. The wood came from an old outbuilding on the property that collapsed."

"I think I will show her the pictures to make sure she knows what it looks like."

"Go for it."

The backup generator whirred to life and she jumped right into him. He steadied her, his hands on her shoulders.

"What's that?" Her eyes wide.

"The generator, so we don't blow a fuse when they use all the tools at once."

She stayed there, too close, for a few seconds longer. His cell started up and she stepped back.

Tugging his gaze away from hers, he dug his phone from his pocket, scanned the screen. Wallace Montgomery. The architect he and Tuckerman once worked with. He jogged away from the generator before answering.

"Brock McBride here. Good to hear from you, sir."

Wallace chuckled. "You still have me in your phone after all these years. I'll take that as a compliment."

"You're one of the best I ever worked with."

"Same here, which is why I called. I've got an opportunity to design luxury cabins for an upscale resort in Fredericksburg. Wondered if you might be on board to work with me."

"I'm surprised you'd want to work with me again." Brock focused on the wildflowers dancing in the slight breeze. "After the way things went down before."

"The problem in that partnership was Tuckerman. You're the most skilled builder I've ever worked with. Honest and reliable to boot."

"I appreciate that, sir." Relief washed over him. Maybe

his reputation wasn't completely in shreds. "I'm afraid I might be tied up for the next few months, but after that..."

"It'll be August at least. I'll call again when we get a definite timeline."

"Thank you, sir. It'll be a privilege to work with you again." Brock hung up, turned around.

Devree stood right in front of him.

"Sorry. I wasn't trying to listen in. Just frantic to escape the racket before it drives me completely buggy." But there was a dullness in her eyes. "You've got a job opportunity?"

"Yeah. I thought I'd blown it the last time we worked together, but apparently not."

"Thanks for putting it off for Chase and Landry." She slipped her hands in her back pockets. "Is there anything I can do to help speed completion along here at the house?"

"The ceiling will be old rusty tin. It all has to get several coats of polyurethane to meet code. You can help me with that." He expected her to decline. She wanted the work done, but did she want to get her hands dirty?

No answer. She headed to her car.

"Guess I'll take that as a no."

"Actually, I'm going to change clothes. Be right back." She glanced over her shoulder at him.

And his heart did a funny thing in his chest. This could easily get out of hand. Who was he trying to kid? It was already out of hand.

Chapter Eleven

Devree parked her car in the lot and hurried to the ranch house, mentally cataloguing her supply of work clothes. Definitely lacking in that area. But she and Landry were the same size—at least until the pregnancy. Maybe she could borrow something.

As the door shut behind her, she stopped. In the foyer, she found Becca pacing.

"What's wrong?"

"There's a man in the office applying for the handyman position."

Her heart sank to the pointy toes of her high heels. "Maybe Chase won't hire him."

"He will if this guy is qualified at all. Brock has made it abundantly clear he's only here as a favor." Becca wrung her hands. "I thought this was my chance to get reacquainted with my son. If he leaves now, I'll probably never see him again."

"I can't believe that. Surely God put you both here at the same time for a reason." Devree slipped an arm around Becca's thin shoulders. "Say this guy gets hired. Chase and Brock have rediscovered their friendship. I bet if Brock ends up leaving, he'll come back to visit. Especially when the baby's born."

"I just need time. To chip away at his armor. Soften his heart. And find my place in it again."

"We'll have to hope the applicant is underqualified. Or overqualified for that matter."

"But then that makes me feel bad." Becca went back to pacing. "What if this man really needs the job?"

"You're so sweet. Always putting others before yourself."

Becca scoffed. "I try. But believe me, it used to be all about me."

The conversation she'd overheard in the chapel popped into her brain unbidden. What was Becca's secret? None of her business. Something for Brock and his mom to work out among themselves.

"You go on about what you need to do. Don't let me hold you up."

"I just came to borrow some work clothes from Landry, so I can polyurethane rusty tin."

"Not exactly in your event planner job description."

"No, but it'll speed completion on the new house, so I'm up for it. Tell you what, I'll go change and then I'll wait here with you."

"You don't have to do that."

"How long can an interview take? Not long enough to make a big difference in my schedule. Be right back." She headed to the great room.

No Landry. She crossed to her sister's suite, silently turned the knob, pushed the door open. Dark inside. Her eyes adjusted to the dimness enough to make out the form of her sister in the bed. Lying on her side, the heaviness of her abdomen propped on a pillow. Devree tiptoed across to the closet, stepped inside, shut the door.

With the small light flipped on, she felt like an inter-loper sifting through Landry's clothes. She found the jeans all hung together. She grabbed a paint-splotched pair with a pink T-shirt in the same condition and pulled both from the rack.

Minutes later, she stepped from the closet dressed in Landry's clothes. Though they were practically the same size, the jeans were a bit loose in the waist. Should have thought to grab a belt, but she was halfway to the door when Landry mumbled something in her sleep. She'd have to make do.

She stopped in her tracks until Landry quieted. Look-ing for a belt wasn't worth waking her sister over. She'd find hay twine or something and pull an Elly May Clamp-pett. Tiptoeing, she made it to the door and out without disturbing her sister.

A whimper came from the couch. Becca sat there, shoulders slumped, face in her hands.

Oh, no. Chase had hired the new handyman. Brock would be leaving. Emotion clogged in her throat. Why did she care? Empathy for Becca? Yes. But mostly because, despite her best efforts, she'd developed feelings for him.

"I'm so sorry, Becca." She sat down beside his dis-traught mom.

Becca raised her head, dabbed under her eyes with her thumbs. "Sorry. I just needed a moment to pull myself together."

"Are you sure Chase hired the guy?"

"I was in the foyer when they came out of the office. Chase took him out to show him around, said he could start first thing in the morning."

Her eyes stung. More than anything, she wanted to cry with Becca. "Maybe you can get Brock's number before he leaves. And I'm working with him most days. I'll try to convince him to talk to you before he leaves."

"No, don't." Becca grabbed Devree's wrist. "That will only make him angry at you. He'll probably have to give notice. I'll try to meet with him before he leaves. See if I can't make some headway to repair our relationship."

"Becca." Ron hurried to her side. "What's wrong?"

"Oh, Ron." Becca dissolved into tears.

Devree quickly explained the situation to Ron, then left them alone. Back to spread polyurethane on rusty tin. Side by side with Brock. Would Chase tell him the news with her there? Would she have to pretend she was pleased? While all she wanted to do was beg him to stay. Not for Becca's sake. But for her own.

Cup of coffee to his lips, Brock stood in the doorway of the wide galley between the barn stalls. He needed to get to the new house for day two of poly on tin. Devree was probably already there. Maybe it would be tolerable if she clammed up today the way she had yesterday.

But today was different than any other day of the year and he always felt closest to his dad here. Memories of him repairing the stalls, the roof, the slatted flooring in the loft. Letting Brock *help*. Dad's birthday had driven him here this morning.

"You always loved coming to the barn with him." Mom behind him. "Happy birthday, Wesley."

The quiver in her voice forced him to face her. So she did remember.

Chin trembling, she clamped a hand over her mouth, sank to a hay bale. "I loved him so much. So much, I couldn't function when I lost him. Even though you needed me. I just wasn't strong enough. Especially after I lost our apartment and we had to move in with your grandfather."

Her obvious pain drew him to her. The only person on earth who missed his dad as much as he did. He settled beside her on the hay bale, could feel the racking sobs she held back in his heart.

"I'm so sorry." She leaned into him. "Your grandfather was always in his alcoholic stupor, feeling no pain. I wanted to feel that way, just once. Just for a little while until I could get a handle on things." Her words ended on a sob, followed by a long pause.

He put his arm around her, absorbed her shudder.

"I didn't want to end up like my dad. So there was this guy at the motel where I cleaned. I knew he dealt drugs." She shrugged. "I thought I could handle it. Just once. But I was hooked before I knew what hit me. Isn't that the stupidest thing? I didn't want to end up an alcoholic, so I tried drugs instead."

Words failed him.

"I let you down. And you're right, I did abandon you. But I didn't mean to. I loved you. I still do." She raised up, looked at him. "I'm so proud of the man you've become. With absolutely no help from me." She scoffed.

"You got the wind knocked out of you. We both did."

"But we survived. I have Ron and a chance to make things right with you. I hope."

And he had memories of his dad. No woman to love. No family. Except this woman he'd spent so many years hating.

"If I'd had God back then, things would have been so very different."

"Maybe He's giving us a fresh start."

"I'd like to make the most of it." She sniffled. "How much longer will you be here?"

He frowned. They'd taken a step forward together this morning. But he wasn't sure he'd stay permanently. "I'll stick with the original plan. Until Chase hires a new handyman or the baby's born. Whichever comes first."

"But I thought he hired someone yesterday."

"Oh, yeah. I heard about that. He wasn't qualified. But he had experience as a hunting guide and a ranch hand, so Chase hired him for that."

Mom pressed her face into his shoulder, blubbered unintelligibly.

"Even if Chase found someone to replace me, I'd give two weeks' notice." His arm tightened around her. "I'd be here for that length of time no matter what."

"So, do I still have to stay away from you?"

"No. You stink at it, anyway." He eased her away from him and stood. "I'll see you around, but right now I gotta get to work."

"Please give me a second chance. I won't blow it this time."

"We'll see." He strode away, a mix of emotions roiling in his gut.

His dad's death hurt her as much as it did Brock, and she loved him with a mother's love. But the abyss of their years apart still yawned between them.

Devree rolled thick gooey polyurethane on a piece of tin that looked like it needed to be condemned. But Landry loved all things rustic, even the mismatched wood in the den. And Devree would do whatever it took to keep her sister happy and stress-free.

Which meant continuing to work side by side with Brock. Every day she felt closer to him as every day brought them closer to going their separate ways.

But where was he this morning? He was usually here by now. Was he consulting with the new guy? Would the new handyman be as agreeable to work with as Brock had been? Or would he think helping her hang curtains and wall art was beneath him?

But more pressing was that when Brock left…she'd miss him. Only days ago, he'd kissed her. And she'd shot him down. He'd been all business since then.

It wouldn't have worked, anyway. Her heart was in Dallas. And Brock's could never survive there. It was best that it ended. She just needed to get through however long of a notice he'd given Chase and maybe her heart would one day go back to normal.

With her long extension pole, she dipped back into the goo, rolled off the excess.

"Sorry I'm late."

She chanced a glance up.

His face looked drawn, haggard.

Maybe, deep down, he really didn't want to leave. "Are you okay?"

"Today would have been my dad's fiftieth birthday."

"I'm sorry." Pushing her topsy-turvy emotions aside, she set down the extension pole and placed her hand on his arm.

"I was in the barn." His shoulders sagged. "He made lots of repairs there when I was a kid and let me hang out with him. It was our place."

"I'm glad you're here. Where you can feel close to him."

"My mom showed up."

"How did that go?"

"I've been angry with her for so long." He picked up his roller, sank it in the poly. "But we talked. It was nice."

"I'm so glad. Everyone needs family."

"Can you keep a secret? Even from Landry and Chase."

"As long as it won't hurt them, I won't tell anyone. I promise."

"It won't. It's ancient history." He sighed, long and hard.

"My mom got hooked on drugs after we left here. I was raised, and not raised, by a series of foster parents from the time I was ten. Some good, some bad." He grimaced. "Some really bad."

"I'm so sorry. I had no idea." Devree tried to hold in her shock. Act like the bomb he'd just dropped was no big deal.

"She told everyone here, after she got out of drug rehab, that I was with my dad's family. That they turned me against her. Covering her tracks."

"I can see why you've been so angry with her." She leaned on her paint-roller rod. "And I'm honored that you trust me enough to talk about it."

"She told Chase's grandmother her secret, but that truth died with Granny—that's what everybody called her. Not even Ron knows about the drugs. But today, I got a glimpse of how much Dad's death truly devastated her." He swallowed hard. "And it hit me, we were both dealt a really bad blow when he died. My bitterness toward her is hurting me as much as her. And we've both had enough pain."

"It's really good that y'all are talking things out. For both of you. You need each other."

"I can't stay here and keep her secret though. When I first came, she promised to work up the courage to tell Ron the truth." He let out a harsh laugh. "I mean, imagine family dinners. Say, Ron asks me if I played basketball in school and I have to tell him that I was never with one family long enough to be under one coach and learn the rules of the game."

"Just give her time." With all his ambivalence toward his mother, he wore his hurt like a cloak. And she longed to comfort him. But her words came out sounding like platitudes. "I'm sure she's scared of how he'll take the news and what he'll think of her."

"Does it change your opinion of her?"

She thought for a moment. Of how kind and supportive Becca had always been. "No. Your mother is very sweet. I won't pretend everything you've told me isn't a shock. But her past is her past. And if anyone else had told me about it, I probably wouldn't have believed them. That's a reflection on the person she is now."

He gave a curt nod at her statement. "I'm holding up production," he said, obviously wanting to change the subject. He rolled his dripping paint rod, sloughed off the excess and spread the coating on the tin.

All she wanted to do was hug him. The parentless child he'd been. And the hurting man he was now. Instead, she rolled the sealant on her piece of tin and said a prayer of comfort for him.

"So since you made progress with your mom, are you still planning to leave?"

"Guess you heard about the new hire too. The guy didn't know a pipe wrench from a crescent."

"A common mistake. They both have those adjusty things." She tried to keep it cool, as if the new hire had no effect on her. That it didn't matter one iota if Brock stayed or left.

"Adjusty things, huh?" He grinned. "Anyway, turns out he had experience in other areas Chase was looking to hire for."

The combo of his knee-jolting smile and her own relief clogged her brain. She didn't hear exactly what the new hire's job description entailed. Didn't care. "So, you're staying?"

"For the time being."

The most beautiful words she'd heard. In weeks. A reprieve. Their time together would still come to an end. But not yet at least.

* * *

Surrounded by freshly painted sage green walls and crib parts, Devree peered at the directions.

"Need some help?" Brock leaned in the doorway.

"Why does it have to be so confusing?"

"It makes it a challenge." He settled beside her, his knee almost touching hers, took the instructions from her and focused on them.

After a few minutes, he sorted the pieces into neat stacks. A bit more reading and he picked up two pieces, fit them together, then screwed them in place. "What about kids?" He looked up at her.

"What about them?"

"Ever picture yourself having any?"

"I've always wanted a couple." Her heart sank a little at the admission as she'd pretty much given up on that dream.

"How do you reckon that can happen if a relationship isn't in your plan?"

"So are you a relationship expert?"

"Hardly." He assembled two more pieces. "After my dad died—my family was splintered. Since then, I've always wanted a family of my own. A do-over—the chance to get it right."

"Any progress on that?"

"Not so far." A harsh laugh escaped him. "I fell hard once, even got engaged."

So he did have experience in the prospective groom department. Was he still hung up on his ex-fiancée? "What happened?"

He joined another piece of the crib in place. "I worked with her father. He and I didn't agree on some of his business practices, so I got out. She took his side in the matter. Chose her dad and to live in Austin over me."

"I'm sorry."

"I'm over it. For the most part. What about you?"

She blew out a big breath.

"I'm not buying that it's all because of the country's divorce rate. You mentioned there was a guy who broke things off with you."

Her gaze settled on the floor. "That's not exactly accurate."

"Care to share?"

"I've never talked about it with anyone."

"Not even Landry?"

"It was too fresh at first and by the time I wanted to dump on her, her doctor couldn't detect her first baby's heartbeat and she was rushed to delivery. But it was too late." She swallowed the knot in her throat. "After that, my disastrous dating saga was trivial."

"But it still hurt you. Come on, I told you my tale of woe. See if you can top me."

"Oh, but I can." Her tone turned bitter, as she fiddled with a pack of screws. "I had a phone consultation with a bride-to-be. She hired me and we met to talk about the wedding. When I walked in, she was sitting with...with my boyfriend. He was the groom."

Brock let out a long, slow whistle, set down the pieces of the crib he'd assembled.

"I was so stupid."

"No. He was a jerk. Did you tell the bride?"

She scoffed. "I didn't have to. He took one look at me and got all weird. She knew something was up and asked me if I knew him."

"It sounds like one of those soap operas my eighth foster mom used to watch when I was a kid."

How many foster families had he had? "I apologized and told her that after rechecking my schedule, I'd overbooked myself and couldn't do their wedding. Before I could escape, she got in his face, demanded to know what was going on between him and the wedding planner. I hightailed it out of there before it got any more heated. Needless to say, they never made it to the altar."

Why had she just dumped all that on him? A guy she'd known only a matter of weeks.

"I don't understand. Why would he do such a thing?"

She shrugged, tried to keep her tone matter-of-fact. "Apparently, he really liked me, but she was from a wealthy family. He thought he could have his cake and eat it too. Didn't work out for him at all."

The whole thing with Randall had been embarrassing, but she hadn't loved him. Her boyfriend drama paled in comparison to his trauma with his mother.

"You win."

Laughter bubbled up and escaped from her in a high-pitched giggle. And she couldn't seem to stop. It was such a relief to talk about it after all this time. Especially since Brock hadn't judged her for being naive and too trusting. Finally, she got a reign on her hilarity, clamped her mouth shut.

"I'm sorry." His hand covered hers. "You deserve better."

"Thanks. You do too."

"At least I'm willing to keep trying." Green eyes pulled at her. He picked up two large constructed pieces of the crib, fit them together and screwed them in place.

She scooted over a bit, put some space between them. Even though they'd bonded over their hurts, they had nothing in common. He was as country as she was city. There was no other way for it to go. They'd end up parting ways.

In the meantime, they needed to remain on separate paths.

No matter how appealing Brock McBride was. No matter how perfect his kiss. No matter how the neglected child inside him tugged at her.

Chapter Twelve

"I promise, there are absolutely no fumes," Devree whispered to Chase, even though Landry was sound asleep in the back seat. Her sister had had to go into the hospital after experiencing some contractions, but it had been a false alarm.

Still, Devree and Brock had picked up the pace on finishing up Landry and Chase's home. Which they would move into soon if Chase could just trust her.

"I had Becca come smell and you know what a good nose she has."

"I don't want to drive her over there, get her hopes up and the smell still be strong—affect her in some negative way. Let's just wait until Monday like we planned."

"It's been four days since the painters were here. Trust me, the house is ready and don't you think she'll rest and relax better here?" Devree glanced back at her sister. "She's sound asleep. I'll stay in the car with her while you go look around. If she wakes up, I'll tell her you had to check on something. If you're not convinced, we'll go back to Granny's old room at the ranch lickety-split and wait it out a few more days."

"All right." Chase turned into the drive, continued

past the ranch house, down the winding road to his and Landry's dream home.

It really was lovely, she thought as they neared the grove of live oaks where the driveway disappeared. A few more yards of woods, shaded with a clearing around the house. Log on the outside, drywall on the interior walls. Farmhouse and rustic decor. A perfect mixture of her sister and the man she loved.

Devree glanced back at Landry as Chase parked, quietly opened his truck door, got out and pushed it to. Landry didn't stir.

Chase disappeared inside. Minutes ticked past. And she started to worry. It wasn't imperative that Landry move in right away. But it sure would help her outlook. She'd rest better without dude ranch guests around and Chase had relinquished his duties until the baby was born. However, he was so overcautious. If he detected the slightest hint of paint fumes, he'd nix the whole idea.

The front door opened and Chase came out. As Devree held her breath, he gave her a thumbs-up. Her smile spread from ear to ear.

He opened the back door, tried to rouse Landry. "Sweetheart, we're home."

Landry opened her eyes for a second as Devree got out.

"It's time to move into the new house." Chase kissed Landry's cheek. "Want to sleep in our new bedroom tonight?"

Landry's eyes opened again. She looked around and her mouth formed a small *o*.

"All ready to move in."

"Really?"

"Yep, scoot over here so I can carry you across the threshold."

Landry sat up, gingerly moved over to the edge of the seat and Chase scooped her up.

"Get a picture, Devree." Landry beamed over her husband's shoulder.

Devree dug her phone out, snapped several pictures.

"You did this, didn't you?" Landry wiped a tear.

"Along with Brock, a whole carpentry crew and every ranch hand on the place. Every stick of furniture, every picture, every doodad should be right where you wanted it."

"You're the best sister ever."

"Right back at ya."

Chase opened the door and Devree snapped one final shot. "I'll text them to you."

"Aren't you coming in?" Chase turned back to face her.

"She needs to rest and y'all don't need me hanging around. I'll stop in tomorrow."

Landry blew her a kiss and the door closed.

Oh, to have a love like that. A man so tender and caring. So completely devoted.

"Psst."

With a confused frown, Devree turned around.

Brock leaned out from behind a tree. "I wanted to see her face."

"She was thrilled."

"I noticed." He held his hand up for a high five.

Sparks flew at the impact of her palm against his.

"Want a ride back to the ranch house? I parked on the other side of the grove there." His gaze dropped to her feet. "I figured you'd have your usual footwear on. Not good for a trek that far."

Thoughtful and caring. "Sure."

She didn't need a man *like* Chase. She needed Brock.

But from all indications, he'd never leave his beloved countryside...not even for her.

Brock rang the bell of the new house, hoping not to disturb Landry. But his boss had summoned him here.

The door swung open revealing a tired-looking Chase. "Just the guy I needed to see. It's Saturday, May 12."

Brock frowned, searching for the significance. The day before... "Do you need me to pick up a Mother's Day gift for your mom or Landry?"

"No. I'm on top of that." Chase waved him inside. "But Mom called and reminded me the annual Medina River cleanup is today. With everything going on, I forgot all about it. She and Dad volunteered to provide the fixings and sides for the barbecue. Can you help them set up and serve?"

"Sure. What time?"

"They serve from five to seven. Probably set up at four."

"Can I get in on the cleanup too?"

"That would be great. Landry and I usually volunteer, so you and Devree can fill our spot. She's already here. I'd arranged for her to stay with Landry, while I went. But the other day's contractions convinced me to bail."

Brock almost swallowed his tongue. A tug-of-war raged inside him. The longing lodged in his heart to spend the day with her while his brain said to run while he still could. He needed to avoid her. Keep his heart safe from her charms.

Chase rushed into the living room. "Devree, I don't mean to *chase* you off, but the cleanup starts soon."

"I'm going, I'm going." She stood, noticed Brock, went still.

"I'll load the canoe."

"Wait! Canoe?" Devree trailed after Chase. "I don't

know how to canoe. Can't I just walk along the shore and clean?"

"Other people are doing that. Devree and I always take the canoe. But no worries, Brock is going with you. He knows how."

Her eyes went wide. Then met his. Obviously wishing she hadn't agreed. Welcome to the club. The rational part of him didn't want to spend the day with her any more than she wanted to hang with him.

"You good with getting wet in what you're wearing?" Chase asked.

Brock considered his shorts, T-shirt and tennis shoes. Work clothes that could use a good dunking. "I'm good. I'll help with the canoe." He followed Chase into the garage where Devree's storage trailer was parked inside.

They tugged a long boat hauler to Brock's truck and hitched it in place, then trekked back to the garage. Each of them grabbed an end of the canoe, lowered it off the wooden brackets on the wall. Brock backed his end out toward his truck.

By the time it was loaded, sweat trickled down Brock's back. Splashing around in the river would be welcomed. Just not with Devree.

"Thanks for helping with this." Chase turned back to the house.

"No problem." He headed for his truck just as Devree exited the front door.

She scurried his way, climbed up in his cab. "Maybe I can catch a canoe with someone else."

He'd love to take her up on that. But... "I think since you're inexperienced, we should stick together." He started the engine, backed out of the drive, headed for the road. "You need to know a bit about canoeing before you hop in one."

"Like?"

"The bow is the front end. The stern is the back."

"Why not just say front and back then?"

Good question. "The person in the stern steers, so you'll need to be in the bow. That way, all you'll have to do is paddle. To keep the canoe straight and steady, each person will paddle on opposite sides of the boat. If you get tired, say *switch* and we'll change sides."

"Sounds easy enough."

"If we come to a turn in the river or we drift too close to the shore, we'll need to paddle on the same side for a little while." He wouldn't go into what to do if they turned sideways or hit the shore. No need to overload her. If he schooled her on the important stuff, the what-ifs wouldn't happen.

"Anything else?"

"Don't stand up once we're out in the water. You'll tip us over if you do. Can you swim?"

"Yes."

"We'll wear life vests, anyway."

"Got it."

They reached the river and he turned into the gravel lot and found a parking spot.

Should be a fun day. Spending it with the one woman he could imagine spending the rest of his life with—but never would.

The canoe swayed beneath her feet as Devree stepped into it.

"Crouch low, keep your weight centered and hold on to both sides until you get to the seat," Brock instructed.

"It keeps moving."

"I've got the canoe, it's not going anywhere until I get in. You don't have motion sickness, do you?"

"No." She inched to the front of the canoe—the bow, that is.

"Good job, you're almost there."

Finally, she settled on the seat, but kept her grip on the sides just in case.

"Perfect. Now just sit still while I get in and push off. Remember what I told you about paddling?"

"I start on the left." She glanced around. A few other canoers gave her reassuring smiles. Was she the only newbie?

The canoe shifted with his weight and suddenly she was propelled forward. She held on white knuckled.

"Paddle, Devree."

Oh, yeah, that. She stuck her oar in the water, pushed back with it, then up and repeat.

"Lengthen your stroke a bit. Don't pull up so quick."

She pushed back, kept her oar in the water longer.

"That's it. You look like a pro. Now, we're clearing out trash and debris from last year's flooding. Use your pinchers while I steer. Don't worry about getting the big stuff. Someone with a bigger boat will handle that part. I may tell you to lean right or left to keep us steady."

This was getting more complicated as they went. Why had she agreed to do this again? There were plenty of people here—a convoy of canoes in front of them. Chase and Landry wouldn't have been missed. There'd been no need for Brock and Devree to take their places. Unless it was a setup. Was Landry trying to matchmake again? Why, oh, why hadn't Devree figured it out before she'd agreed to come?

"See that bottle floating there? Can you get it? Don't lean too much."

She eased her grabber into the water, nabbed the bottle, then pulled it in and dropped it into one of their trash bags.

"Good job. Switch."

She moved her oar to the other side. Much easier since she was right-handed.

She grabbed an aluminum can and several plastic utensils. "Lean right."

A big piece of something glistened to her right up ahead. They neared it and she jabbed her oar at it. Heavy. The boat dipped sideways a bit.

"Leave it. I think it's part of a car or something. One of the bigger boats will get it."

But the canoe was turning sideways.

"Switch," Brock instructed.

The canoe righted itself into a straight line, but nearer the shore than they'd been.

"Switch," he shouted.

She scrambled to follow his command, but movement in a branch too close to the boat caught her attention. Snake. She screamed, jumped up.

"Devree, sit down!"

The boat flipped, tossed her in the water, but her life vest kept her from going under. She swiped at her eyes, searched for the limb where she'd seen the snake and realized she was too close.

She swam away from it. If there were snakes in the trees, they were probably in the river too. And the only kind of snake she knew of that hung around rivers were extremely venomous water moccasins. Her hands hit something solid. She screamed, swatted at the water. But it was Brock.

"Calm down." He grabbed her by the shoulders. "What are you doing?"

"There was a snake on the limb and they're probably in the water."

"They're not poisonous, just water snakes."

"Water moccasins?"

"No. Stop freaking out, so I can swim the canoe to shore and we can get back in it."

She nodded. But something touched her thigh. She kicked and flailed, screamed again.

"I can't get the canoe if I have to hold on to you."

"Something touched my leg. That may have been a water snake in the tree—" she shuddered, though the water was a nice temperature "—but there probably are water moccasins in the river. Right?"

"I've never heard of anyone getting bit by one in the water. Here, hold on to me while I get the canoe."

She reluctantly slipped her arms around his neck. Her fears forcing her to do his bidding.

"No flailing around, okay? You're fine. I'll get you back in the canoe if you'll work with me."

She held on tight, bit her lip until she tasted blood, as he swam the canoe to shore. As they neared the tree line, he was walking. She should get down, but she held on like the big scared ninny that she was.

"You can walk now. I can see the bottom. There aren't any snakes. None on the shore, either."

She put her feet down, let go of him. "Sorry. I can't tell you how much I hate snakes."

"Would have been nice to know before I got in a canoe with you on a river where snakes have been known to hang around." He grinned, dragged the boat ashore, tilted it on its side. Once the water drained out, he turned it upright.

"Ready to get back in?"

"Are there any alternatives?"

"Walking back to the truck."

Thick overgrowth lined most of the shore on each side.

"I'll hold it steady while you get in like before."

A whimper escaped at the prospect, but she climbed

in, hunkered low, held on and made her way to the seat in the bow.

"I'll get you down the river in one piece. I promise. You're doing great. I'm getting in now." The canoe shifted with his weight and they propelled forward. "Paddle on the left until we get her straightened out."

The boat glided to the middle of the river, then turned to go with the flow.

"Switch."

"We lost all the trash we picked up."

"Someone else will get it. I have a feeling we'll do good just to get to the other end intact."

"How will we get back to your truck?"

"Volunteers are waiting. They'll take us back."

This debacle certainly hadn't endeared her to him. "I'm really sorry."

"It's okay. We'll do our part when it comes time to dole out the food."

Just get across the river without flipping them again. Another few hours and this torture of being with him would be over. Then maybe they could work in separate cottages. Until her niece or nephew, Sprint, was born and she found the courage to leave him behind.

Brock helped carry the portable buffet warmers to the long line of tables set up. Tray after tray of baked beans and corn on the cob. Iced down coolers held vats of coleslaw and potato salad.

"What do we charge?" he heard Devree ask. "Since I'm at the end of the line, am I responsible for the money?"

"It's free." Chase's mom said as she handed out dippers and tongs.

"Free? I guess it brings in customers."

"I hadn't really thought about that." Janice shrugged. "We just do it because it's a good thing for the community."

Devree really had a lot to learn about country life. But he knew she wouldn't stick around long enough for that.

"What about drinks?"

"Someone else is providing those. I can't remember who." Janice bustled around, stirring the hot dishes.

"This part's much easier than canoeing." Elliot patted Devree's shoulder. "You got this." Chase's dad always had a great sense of humor about everything.

She chuckled. "Hey, I managed to fill a trash bag."

She was always a good sport about getting ribbed. At ease with everyone but him it seemed. Yet, when she'd over-turned their canoe and was so scared, all he wanted to do was protect her. Tell her that he'd keep her safe forever... if she'd let him.

But they couldn't build a relationship, not with her long-ing to return home and reinvent her business in Dallas. And even if she stayed, she'd never fit in around here, never be happy. He knew from experience with his mom and dad that if he asked her to stay she would probably end up resenting him.

"You're on slaw duty." Janice handed him a slotted spoon.

Right next to Devree and the potato salad. "Let's pray," the cleanup coordinator shouted. Everyone bowed their heads. He couldn't make out most of the words, but after a few minutes, a round of amens moved through the crowd.

The line started up and he plopped coleslaw on count-less plates, bumped elbows with Devree a few times. As usual, the slightest touch sent a shock through him.

Eventually, the end of the line came and they served the last volunteer.

"Maybe we'll have time to eat before the volunteers

from the other routes get here." Janice jabbed a dish at him, then Devree.

They filled their plates in silence.

Brock glanced around. A boy scout troop played a rousing game of touch football in the distance. Volunteers lined long tables that had been set up with folding chairs, along with picnic blankets and canvas seating. Tents lined the parking lot since many had camped last night.

"Where do we sit?" She looked around. "Were we supposed to bring chairs?"

"I brought a blanket for us." Elliot spread a bright quilt on the ground. "There's plenty of room."

He and Janice settled on one side, leaving him and Devree the other. As if they were a couple. Was all of Bandera out to drive him to distraction, intent on keeping her near him?

Since things were easier with his mom, he wasn't itching to go like he'd been before. Maybe he could stick around, repair things further between them. But having Devree near kept him off-kilter. Even if he stayed, she definitely wouldn't.

"Here, I'll hold your food while you sit." He took the dish from her.

"Thanks." She settled on the quilt, then took both plates from him.

His knee grazed hers as he joined her. "Sorry."

"Oh, look." Janice set her hand on Elliot's calf. "More volunteers from one of the other routes. We better get back to the buffet line."

Elliot helped her up. "Y'all stay and eat. There aren't many. We can handle them."

And here they were, alone again. Like a date. But it wasn't and never could be. He searched for something to say. A band started up from a flatbed trailer at the edge of the river.

"So, since you and Becca are getting along better, do you think you'll stay in Bandera?" She'd beat him to it.

"Maybe so. I like it here."

"No offense to your dad's line of work, and handyman is an honorable and much-needed profession, but I saw the magazine Becca had. You're way overqualified and over-talented."

Another lifetime ago. It seemed like it, anyway. "I'll admit, working in the cabins has made me itch to build them again. Once Chase no longer needs me, I have an opportunity to get back into cabin design."

"And still stay here?"

"I'm willing to travel, but my home base could be Bandera."

"I'm glad. I mean—that you're sticking around—for your mom's sake. And yours."

"What about you? Are you planning to leave as soon as Landry has the baby?"

"I may stay a few days after until they get settled."

Hadn't anticipated that. He'd expected her to be gone ASAP. But she did love her sister.

An elderly couple strolled over. "Are you Devree Malone?"

"Yes." She set her plate aside and stood.

"Wonderful. A lady told us you're an event planner in Dallas."

"That's right."

"Oh, good." The woman patted her husband's arm. "I'm Gladys Hewitt and this is my husband. Stanley and I live there and our sixtieth anniversary is in August. Our kids are planning a big party on the twelfth, but we'd like to remove the burden from them, so they can enjoy it too."

Brock stood. "I'll find some chairs for y'all."

"We have some—the two red ones by that big cypress tree." The man pointed, and Brock went to fetch the them. "Thank you, young man."

Minutes later, Brock set the chairs up for them. "I'll let y'all talk planning."

"You don't have to leave," Devree protested.

"Might as well get used to going in different directions."

She blinked. "Thanks for the chairs."

He strolled away, wishing he could leave right now and drive back to the ranch. But he'd brought her here and even though she could ride back with Janice and Elliot, he'd never been the type to shuck his duties off on someone else, and he wouldn't start now.

Dallas was already calling her home. Maybe once she left, his chest would stop with the constant ache.

Chapter Thirteen

Devree scrolled through her calendar on her phone, but she was too distracted to focus. Was Brock eager for her to leave? It sure seemed like it. From the moment she'd agreed to stay at the dude ranch and help out until Sprint was born, she'd counted down the days until she could go home. But now, that meant leaving Brock behind.

Obviously, Brock didn't feel the same way. Something jabbed deep in her chest.

"Do you have the date open, dear?" Mrs. Hewitt pressed.

"Let me just check something." She scrolled to August. "I have the twelfth."

"Perfect." Mrs. Hewitt clapped her hands.

"Do you have a venue?"

"We already booked the Empire Room in Dallas for that day."

"Nice. I'll put you on my calendar. What do you say we meet there toward the end of next month and talk specifics?"

"That sounds great. I'm so glad we happened upon you."

They settled on a time.

Devree wrote the details on the back of her business

card then handed it to Mrs. Hewitt. "What brings y'all to Bandera?"

"Both our families are from here. This is where we met and fell in love." Mrs. Hewitt looked at her husband, obviously as love-struck as she'd been when they were young. "Our jobs took us to the city. We always planned to return to Bandera, but then the kids settled in Dallas. So we come back every year for the cleanup."

"We help supply drinks." Stanley winked at his wife. "And Gladys brings a cobbler. She makes a mean cobbler."

Their affection for one another was so strong and vibrant that Devree could feel it. The kind of love she'd longed for. If she could have acclimated to living in Bandera, could she have had that with Brock? She'd never know since he obviously wasn't interested. Her throat constricted as a painful knot settled in.

"Sorry we ran your young man off." Gladys stood. "Let's leave the happy couple alone, Stanley."

"We're not—" Her words stalled. They weren't together, but she wanted to be.

As soon as Brock saw the Hewitts getting up, he headed back over. "Leaving already? Not on my account, I hope."

"Not at all." Stanley folded his chair, picked it up. "It's past our bedtime."

"I'll get the chairs. Just show me where your car is."

"Such a nice young man." Gladys patted his cheek, then waved at Devree. "We'll see you in Dallas next month."

"See you then."

Brock followed them to the parking lot. A few minutes later, she spotted him returning. More volunteers streamed in from another river route. She and Brock were destined to have their short time left together interrupted. Probably for the best.

She headed to the buffet line to help.

"Janice, y'all never got to eat." Brock claimed his spot beside her. "We'll take this round. You and Elliot get a fresh plate and get some grub."

"I guess we should have eaten in shifts. Now we've wasted food." Elliot filled new helpings for them.

"I think there's plenty." From what she understood, there was only one more river route of volunteers who hadn't arrived yet.

Janice and Elliot left and the line of hungry volunteers trickled to an end.

Scarlet, Ruby and Drew brought up the rear.

"I'm so glad you're here." Scarlet looked like she wanted to hug Brock. "This is my husband, Drew. I've been wanting y'all to meet."

Brock offered his hand. "Nice meeting you."

"You too. Did you eat plenty?"

"Too much." He patted his stomach. "But I'm still planning to dig into that cobbler." He shot Ruby a wink. "When are you coming for your private tour of the petting zoo?"

"I've been wanting to. Maybe this week."

He grinned at Scarlet. "Bring her anytime."

"Thanks."

The family moved on. Definite camaraderie there. Maybe someday, they'd all sit around a big table and share a holiday celebration together. Brock needed that. And Scarlet obviously longed for it.

"I'm diving into this cobbler while I can." Brock grabbed a bowl. "Want some?"

"Yes. The lady I was talking to earlier, Gladys Hewitt, made it. They grew up here and come back every year for the cleanup."

"They seemed really nice. Did you take the job?"

"I did. I'm meeting with them next month at the Empire. It's an event venue in Dallas."

"Believe it or not, I've been there. That's where my wedding was supposed to be."

"I'm sorry." Her heart pinged at the thought of him loving someone else that much.

"I'm not. She was the wrong woman, and it definitely wasn't my kind of place." He closed his eyes. Savoring a bite of cobbler? Or remembering his heartache?

The Empire Room drove home their differences once again. She loved it. He hated it.

"Looks like you'll have plenty to do once you get back to Dallas."

Apparently, that's where he wanted her. And not a moment too soon. She'd had her chance with him and she'd blown it. No do overs.

She'd just have to put on her big girl heels, wait for baby Sprint's arrival and then hightail it back to her life in Dallas. Whether she wanted to or not. She could not stay here and pine over him.

Exhausted, Devree stifled a yawn as she drove to her sister's house. Between all that rowing and the tension with Brock yesterday, she was toast. At least she'd slept well last night. She checked her watch.

Thirty minutes before Sunday school class. Not long to visit with Landry, but her sister had called and begged her to stop by. And she couldn't say no. As she neared the house, she noticed movement on the porch. Someone swinging in a hammock over to the right. Landry.

With a grin, she parked and got out.

"See what Chase got me for Mother's Day?" Landry's head popped up. "Isn't it wonderful? Now, I can at least come outside to lay around."

"I wish it would stay cool enough all day."

"You know me. Heat doesn't bother me like it does you."

The front door whipped open as Mama and Daddy spilled out of the house. "Surprise!"

Devree gasped, then hugged them both. "When did y'all get here?"

"Late last night, after both you girls were already in bed."

"I couldn't be away from y'all on Mother's Day." Mama gave Devree another hug. "Especially since Landry's about to be a mom again." Mama gasped as she apparently realized the implication of her words. "But not like last time. Not at all."

A reverent silence crackled with heaviness. None of them would ever forget little Landon Charles.

Landry scooted over, patted the hammock. "Get in with me."

"What? I'll flip you."

"No, you won't. It's like the one Mama and Daddy have on their porch in Aubrey. We used to lay in it all the time when we were kids."

"The emphasis being on the word *kids*." Daddy chuckled.

"Come on, Chase got in with me last night. It's quite sturdy."

"Hold it steady for them, Owen," Mama instructed.

Devree eyed the contraption. It was anchored in four places instead of two. She grabbed the side, pushed down on it. Nothing. She'd muss her hair and her dress. But she'd do anything for Landry.

"I've got you." Daddy steadied the side for her.

She slipped off her heels, settled on the side of it, then wiggled over and lay down beside her sister. Giggling ensued at her jerky movements, just like when they were kids.

"It was definitely easier to maneuver around in one of these things when we were younger."

"But I think it's even more fun now." Landry giggled.

"Shhh." Mama pressed a finger to her lips. "Listen."

Horses whinnying, the hooting of an owl, the low murmur of ranch hands, the chatter of birds.

"It sounds like home," Devree admitted.

"I knew it." Landry jabbed a finger at her.

"What?"

"You don't think of Dallas as home anymore."

Hmm. She used to. What had happened to her?

The door swung open. Chase eyed them, holding a tray loaded with glasses of lemonade, each with a bendy straw. "Looks like a passel of trouble to me." He handed the glasses to them. "How did you ever get these two raised, Tina?"

Mama laughed. "With lots of love and giggling."

"We used to lay in Daddy's hammock together when were kids. Even tried to sleep there a few times. But Devree always chickened out and ended up inside."

"Landry was always our nature girl." Mama sipped her lemonade.

"Just don't flip my precious cargo when you leave." Chase set down the tray, settled in a chair.

"You look tired, Dev." Landry leaned up to sip the lemonade then sat it down on a side table.

"Flipping a canoe is hard work." She tasted the lemonade. Just the right amount of sweet and tart. She almost drained the glass before placing it next to her sister's.

Daddy guffawed. "We heard all about it."

"Janice thought she saw some sparks between you and Brock." Landry elbowed her.

"Who's this Brock?" Daddy barked.

Devree's face steamed. There'd been definite sparks—for her, anyway.

"The new handyman," Chase volunteered. "An old friend of mine."

"He was just trying to keep me calm and get me back in the canoe. I don't know what you and Chase were thinking, setting me up in a floating ski."

"You do look tired." Mama leaned over them, giving Devree a good inspection. "Did you sleep okay?"

"I bet you haven't slept since you got here." Daddy winked at her. "Too quiet for you."

"The first few nights were rough. But since then, I've slept like a log the entire time I've been here. Except for the rooster waking me up a few mornings. But he's gone now."

"I knew it. You're a country girl at heart." Mama grinned.

"It's so peaceful here." Landry yawned. "I love the slowed-down lifestyle. Where you get to know your neighbors and people care. A lot like Aubrey. Are you sure country life hasn't grown on you again, Devree?"

These days, she wasn't sure about much.

"Ooh." Landry grabbed Devree's hand, pressed it to the mound of her stomach.

Devree felt a jab from inside and teared up. "Does that hurt?"

"Not really. It's just kind of startling sometimes."

"Let me feel." Mama set her hand next to Devree's.

"I can't wait until he or she gets out here." Landry stretched her back.

"You and me both." Breathing and healthy this time. "Trust me." The movement stopped and Devree checked her watch. "I'd love to hang out with you and Sprint all morning, but I better get to church." She sat up, got her toe hung in the netting. Daddy held the hammock steady, but by the time she was safely on her feet, they were both giggling again.

"We're going with you." Mama grabbed her purse from the porch rail.

Devree's heart squeezed. She hadn't been to church with her parents since she'd lived at home.

"Come back after church."

"We will." She blew her sister a kiss and headed for her car with a troubled mind.

Did she really want to go back to Dallas? It was so peaceful here. And she loved being with her sister. It was so much fun with Mama and Daddy here to see them both instead of one at a time. When her niece or nephew was born, could she really just walk away?

The service ended and Brock headed for the door. He should have sat Mother's Day out. It was torture sitting through the sermon with his stepdad singing the praises of his mom while she withheld a big whopping secret from him.

It brought all his anger toward her freshly to the surface. Undermining the steps toward reconciliation they'd made on his dad's birthday.

At least Ron hadn't exposed him as her son.

"Brock? Is that right?" An older man stopped him, offered his calloused hand. "Jed Whitlow. We met at Rustick's a few weeks back. The missus and I have our own church, but our son works as a hand for the Donovans, so we came here today. Can you help us set up some more tables in the fellowship hall? We've got a bigger crowd than Chase expected."

"Sure. You ended up with Rusty the rooster, didn't you?"

"We did." Jed ambled through the side door toward the fellowship hall as he spoke. "He's beautiful and quite happy in his new home."

"Just watch him if he gets out. He's got an attitude."

"So I hear. How's the construction going here at the Donovans'?"

"Coming along. We have three out of a dozen cabins complete."

They made it to the fellowship hall. Women, including his mother, scurried about the kitchen while the men moved the seating around and grabbed more. He helped carry three tables, set them up with chairs.

"I think that's it." Jed swiped his hands back and forth against each other. "You're gonna stay and eat, aren't you? Chase's dad catered it, so the mothers wouldn't have to work so hard. I can vouch for the cook and it sure smells good."

"Thanks, but my recliner's calling me."

"Well, if I'd known you weren't staying, I wouldn't have made you work."

"I didn't mind. Nice seeing you again, Jed."

"Same here."

He headed for the foyer, then toward the exit. The rushed click of heels sounded behind him.

"Brock, I wish you'd stay," Mom begged.

"I can't." He kept his back to her.

"But I haven't had a Mother's Day lunch with you since you were ten."

He turned on her then. "Wonder why that is?"

"I thought we were okay."

"I can't have a family meal with you and Ron the way you want. Not without him knowing the truth. He might ask me something mundane like how Dad's relatives are. And I have no clue." Because he'd never laid eyes on them in his entire life. At least, that he remembered, anyway.

"Oh, Brock, I'm so sorry."

"You being sorry doesn't fix anything. You need to tell your new little family unit the truth."

"What truth is that?" Ron stepped through the doorway from the sanctuary, his gaze bouncing back and forth between them. Scarlet stood behind him.

Mom sucked in a big breath, nodded. "You're right. It's time. Let's go to your office, Ron. You too, Scarlet. There's something I need to tell you both. Something I should have told y'all years ago."

"You coming?" Ron asked. "Sounds like you're part of all of this?"

"No. I'll let y'all hash it out." He exited, leaving her to clean up her own mess.

At his truck, he hesitated. She was finally doing the right thing. Even though she was being forced into coming clean since Ron overheard their argument, she was finally doing it.

Maybe he should stick around, help her with the fallout. He strode back inside, settled on the back pew and did something he hadn't done since he was ten—said a prayer for his mom.

Even though Devree had a good reason for leaving earlier—taking her sister and Chase a plate, visiting with her parents—she felt bad for not helping with the cleanup in the fellowship hall. As she stepped inside the foyer, Ron rushed from his office and out the exit with Scarlet on his heels. Neither said a word. Odd. Brock came barreling from the sanctuary, stopped when he saw her.

"Is Ron okay?"

"No. I'll see to him. My mom's in the office. Can you stay with her until I get back?"

"Of course." She hurried to the office at the side of the foyer.

Inside, Becca sat hunched, her face in her hands.

"Becca, Brock asked me to stay with you. He went after Ron."

"Oh, Devree. I've made such a mess of things."

"You don't have to tell me anything. I'm just here for support."

"But I need to tell it. I should have fessed up when I came back here fifteen years ago." The story tumbled out of Becca, interrupted only by hiccupped sobs. The grief over Brock's dad, the move to Dallas, losing her apartment, her alcoholic father, the drug use, forgetting where she'd left Brock and child services.

"I'm so sorry, Becca." She'd known some of it, but not the gory details like she did now.

"No one knew. Except Granny Donovan. She hired me when I came back here. Said my story was between me and God. But people knew me here and asked about Brock. So I made up a story about his father's family taking him from me, turning him against me."

Devree patted her shoulder.

"I don't think Granny's advice applied to keeping it from my husband. When Ron and I first started seeing each other, I was afraid my past would scare him off. Once we started getting serious, I didn't want to lose him."

"I'm sure he's shocked, but he loves you."

"He said it's not the drugs or my losing Brock that upset him. It's that I didn't trust him enough to tell him. And he's a big stickler on truth. I don't know if he can ever forgive me. Poor Scarlet was shell-shocked."

"I'm sure Brock and Scarlet will calm Ron down."

"Unless none of them can forgive me."

"They're all Christians. Forgiveness is part of the package." Devree took Becca's hand. "Let's pray about it."

Becca sniffled, nodded.

"Dear Lord, ease this situation. Give Ron, Becca, Scarlet and Brock peace and comfort only You can provide. Help them forgive each other. To love each other. To leave the past behind and embrace the future together. In Jesus's precious name, amen."

"Thank you, Devree." Becca squeezed her hand. "I'm sorry you got tangled up in my drama."

"That's what friends are for."

But only God could fix this.

Chapter Fourteen

Brock caught up with Ron and Scarlet at his truck, the door already open.

"Great, she sent you to plead her case?" Ron stood between his pickup and the open driver's door, leaned his elbows through the window, fists clenched.

"No. I came on my own. I'm the one who challenged her to tell you the truth, so I should be around to support her."

"Why didn't she tell me?" Barely controlled anger writhed in Ron's eyes.

"Dad, listen to him." Scarlet touched Ron's arm. "Becca's been so good to us. Let's just leave her past in the past and move forward. She must be distraught. I'll go see about her." She started toward the church.

"I asked Devree to stay with her."

"Then maybe I'll just go inside and pray."

"It's gonna take a lot of praying," Ron closed his eyes. "She would have kept her secret if I hadn't overheard your conversation."

"She would have told you eventually. It was eating at her." Brock kicked at the gravel with the toe of his boot. "You gotta know she's a different person now. As upset as she is at this moment, I seriously doubt she'd go back to drugs."

"It's not the drug abuse or the parental neglect that gets me. She didn't trust me enough to tell me the truth."

"She probably thought you'd figure she was a bad influence if you knew and wouldn't let her near your teenage daughter." Why was it so easy to defend her?

"I wouldn't have broken things off. I loved her."

"And you still do."

"Of course, I do. I'm just…hurt."

"Then don't run out on her. She needs you to love her. To accept her truth. To forgive her for not telling you sooner." Was he forgiving her too?

"How'd you wind up so smart?"

"I had a Christian foster family." For a while. No need to tell Ron about the difficult years his mother's drug abuse had caused him.

"I'm glad. I'm glad you ended up back here." Ron shut his truck door, strode toward the church.

Brock matched his stride. "Me too." And he actually meant it. Despite the turmoil with Devree.

"My first wife passed away when Scarlet was nine. She always wanted a brother and I always wanted a son. I mean, I could never take the place of your dad, but I'm hoping you'll stick around, build a relationship with your mama. And with me and Scarlet."

"I'd like that."

"Wanna take her out to dinner after evening service?"

"Sure." As he'd counseled Ron to forgive his mom, the words had resonated in his heart. It was time he forgave her too. They couldn't retrieve the past, get back what they'd lost, but they could make up for lost time now.

He opened the glass entry door and Ron went inside, straight to his office.

Mom and Devree sat in front of his desk. Both turned to face them. Ron stepped in, pulled Mom to her feet, wrapped her up in his arms.

"We'll leave you alone." Brock gestured Devree out. "But I'll see you later, Mom. How about we go to the Old Spanish Trail for a Mother's Day supper after evening service?"

"I'd like that. A lot." Tears streamed down Mom's face, but they were obviously happy tears now.

Devree exited and Brock followed.

"Sorry you got mixed up in that."

"It's okay. I'm glad it all worked out. I like happy endings."

"You had guests with you this morning. I didn't mean to keep you away from them."

"My parents."

"Mother's Day. I should have figured that out. Scarlet's in the sanctuary. She got caught up in the vortex too. I should check on her." He wouldn't look at her. Couldn't.

"I returned to help clean the fellowship hall." She stopped. "I better get back there or they'll have it done."

"Go, spend time with your folks. There's plenty of cleanup help. How long has it been since you were with your whole family?" He risked a glance her way.

"A while." Her eyes turned sad. "I think I will go."

He found Scarlet on the front pew. Head bowed. Her head whipped up, as she heard his approach.

"Are they okay?"

"They're hugging it out in the office as we speak."

She blew out a big sigh. "Good."

He strolled up the aisle, sat down beside her. "How about you? You okay?"

"It's a lot to take in. But I think I know why she didn't tell us in the beginning."

"Why's that?" He relaxed his shoulders, stretched his legs out, crossed his ankles in an effort to release some of his pent up tension.

"We needed her so bad. And we put her on a pedestal from the start. It must have been a lot of pressure for her. To measure up to how we saw her." She reached for his hand.

He clasped hers. "I shouldn't have forced her. It was selfish. I refused to lie about my childhood, that's why I wouldn't ever agree to that dinner you kept insisting on. I figured the subject would have come up."

"Since they're okay, I think it's good that we know everything she went through. Makes me love her even more."

"You're a good woman." He squeezed her hand. "We're taking Mom to OST for Mother's Day tonight. Hope y'all can come."

"I wouldn't miss it." She laid her head against his shoulder for a few seconds. "I've been trying to arrange a family dinner since I first laid eyes on you. Are you bringing Devree?"

"No." *Absolutely not.*

"You should. Y'all make a cute couple."

"But we're not. Her life is in Dallas and it turns out, mine's here."

"I thought my life was in San Antonio. Until I met Drew. I can't wait for you to get to know him tonight. He's heard so much about my fantasy brother." She giggled as her cheeks turned pink.

"Careful now. I'd topple right off some pedestal." He shot her a wink. "Didn't you grow up here?"

"I couldn't wait to get away—to live in the city." Her gaze grew distant. "As soon as I graduated high school, I went to San Antonio to get my real estate license. I was happy there. Or I thought I was. Until I came to visit Dad and Becca and met the new ranch hand next door."

"And you're happy in Bandera now?"

"Blissfully. The right man changes everything. Maybe you could be Devree's right man."

"I don't think so." But, oh, how he wished he could.

"Mama." Turning around, they saw Ruby. "You're missing Mother's Day."

"You're right, sweetheart. I am." She stood, caught the little girl's hand. "You coming?"

"Hurry, Uncle Brock. They have yummy pie."

"Right behind you. I've never said no to pie." He followed them to the fellowship hall.

Now that things were fully reconciled with Mom, he'd definitely stay here. It could even be his home base if he got back into building luxury cabins again.

During his partnership, Tuckerman had bullied landowners into selling too low and Brock's reputation had gotten tarnished by association. But apparently enough time had passed, and their old architect was willing to take a chance on him. Could he start over?

Maybe he could—but not with Devree. With jobs stacking up for her in Dallas, she'd never stay here. Never be content in Bandera. There would be no happy ending for them.

Monday morning, back to work. On his hands and knees, Brock locked the tongue and groove hardwood flooring together in the completed cottage. Whoever invented kneepads rocked. His hands were busy, his mind was occupied, so why did Devree keep distracting him as she hung curtains and wall decor?

Because he'd gone and done it. Fallen for another city girl. Though she wasn't as selfish as his mom had been in her youth, or calculating like his ex-fiancée, there was just no getting around Devree's obvious need to start her new business in Dallas.

Why did he always fall for the wrong woman? He was twenty-eight years old. At this rate, he'd never have that do-over he always wanted. His chance of having the perfect family was quickly fading.

"Oh, good. I found you." Mom's voice was panicked. "We need your help."

Devree's cordless screwdriver stopped. "Is Landry okay?"

"She's fine. But the pregnant goat, Polly, is missing. She was tucked away in the most secure stall in the barn. I don't know how she got out, but Troy came to the house looking for you. He said you have a way with goats."

"He has a way with the feed bucket." Devree chuckled, her gaze catching his for a brief moment.

Making his heart take a dive for her all over again. "But that won't work since I don't know where she is."

"The hands have searched the entire place. If they don't find her, they're afraid coyotes will get her and the kid."

"Sounds like it's time for a picnic."

"Why didn't I think of that?" Mom smiled, her eyes going warm at the memories.

Shared memories. Good ones.

Devree scrutinized them. "What am I missing?"

"When Brock was little, I took him on a picnic. Six goats were out that afternoon, but we didn't even know it until they all showed up at our picnic."

"Because they were hungry?"

"They were curious." Brock locked another hardwood plank in place, then stood, brushed off the knees of his jeans. "Goats will investigate anything out of the ordinary. They can't seem to help themselves." He turned to his mom, offering an olive branch. "Got time for a picnic?"

Regret filled her expressive eyes. "Oh, how I wish. But we have a full house of guests and this is my cleaning time while the majority of them are out to lunch. But I'd love a rain check on my day off."

"I can probably manage that."

Her chin quivered like she might burst into tears, but she gathered herself. "In the meantime, I'll send one of the kitchen staff over with a basket and you can take Devree."

His heart kicked into overtime. Did Mom know he had a thing for her? Was this really about the goat?

"I do love a picnic, but I have work to do," Devree sighed, as if she truly longed to go. Obviously for Mom's benefit. "But does it really take two people?"

"Goats are very social." Mom peeked out the window. "Conversation seems to draw them out. Please don't make Brock go on a picnic all alone and talk to himself too. It won't take long," she insisted. "And this is Landry's favorite doe. If anything happens to Polly, she'll be crushed."

The trump card. He could almost literally see Devree caving.

"All right."

"Great. I'll send a basket over ASAP." Mom's gaze pinged back and forth between them. A satisfied smile settled in place and she scurried out.

Was the goat even missing? Or was she onto him and trying to spur things along between him and Devree? Was she trying to help him with his happily-ever-after? If so, she was on the wrong track.

Surrounded by the perfect picnic, Devree tried not to look at the captivating cowboy sitting on the bright table-

cloth in the middle of the field with her. A basket filled
with yummy food fresh from the buffet. No goat in sight.

"We need to talk about something to draw her attention."

Devree searched her brain. They had nothing in common. While she worried about spiders or snakes finding
their picnic, he was perfectly content experiencing nature.
She loved the hustle and bustle of the city, he treasured the
sound of crickets and frogs.

"So what do you plan on doing once you get back to
Dallas?"

That again? Why was he so hung up on her leaving?
His enthusiasm for her departure might just convince her
heart to settle down. "The contest has gotten me several
family and high school reunions, along with a couple of
company retreats and conferences."

"Good. So you got what you wanted."

Not really. "How was the family dinner last night?"

"It was nice." He scanned the field surrounding them.
"This place always felt like home to me, so it's great to be
back. For good."

"I'm so glad. I mean—that you and Becca are working things out. She's a very sweet lady." If only they could
overcome Dallas. A pang lodged in her chest. "The Fletch-
ers and Millers are awesome people. You landed in a pretty
cool family."

"Don't look now. But we have a pregnant goat at ten
o'clock."

"Really? Where did she come from?"

"That thicket of oaks behind the barn. I didn't figure
she'd gone far."

"How do you think she got out?"

"That's the thing. I don't think she did. Someone had
to have let her out."

Please, no. "But Lee's not here, anymore."

"No. But he doesn't live far. Whoever paid the last handyman off could have found someone else to do his dirty work."

"Chase really needs to call the police. Is the goat still coming toward us?"

"Sure is."

"How do you plan on catching her?"

"She'll probably come all the way over, let us feed and pet her. I have a rope. You distract her and I'll slip it around her neck."

Which would bring their time together to an abrupt halt. Yes, they'd be back at the honeymoon cottage with him doing flooring and her working on decor. But their forced conversation would end. She hated this strain between them. Wished the kiss had never happened. But then, she wouldn't have the memory to savor.

Her cheeks heated. Dry grass crunched behind her as the goat approached. At least, she hoped it was Polly.

"Right behind you. No sudden moves." He set a container of watermelon between them. "Hey, Miss Polly. Fancy meeting you here," Brock crooned as if speaking to a child. "Want some of my melon?"

The goat nuzzled the container, stole a slice.

"Can I pet you, Polly?" Devree reached toward her, palm up, non-threatening. "You're a pretty goat. As far as goats go." Her hand made contact on the side of Polly's neck. She didn't flinch, just crunched on her watermelon rind. She had thick wiry gray hair with patches of black and white on her face, ears and feet. For some reason, Devree had expected it to be soft. "You still stink though."

Polly raised up to chew, nuzzled Devree's shoulder, probably leaving a pink streak on her favorite white blouse.

"You haven't smelled stink until you get a whiff of a

buck." Brock smoothed his hand along Polly's back. In one swift motion, he slid a rope over her head. "Gotcha."

The goat didn't seem to mind. Just kept chewing as Devree patted her shoulder. "You're a good girl, aren't you?"

"I reckon I'll get her back to the barn and we can continue our work." Brock stood. "Leave this. I'll come and clean it up later."

"I'll take care of it." She wiped her hands down with sanitizer. "We can take it back to the cottage. Nibble while we work."

"I'll track Chase down, tell him somebody's up to no good again, then meet you there." He led the tethered goat toward the barn.

Her heart slid even farther down the slippery slope, landing at Brock's booted feet. Landry's due date couldn't come fast enough. Devree needed to escape the handsome cowboy's magnetic pull. While she still could.

Brock sent a text to Chase.

Is Landry asleep?

No.

Brock dialed the number.

"Your mom suggested I bring plates for y'all. I'm calling to take your order."

"I can come get food." Chase chuckled. "Trust me, I won't go hungry."

"But if I bring it, then you can stay with her." And give him a reprieve from working with Devree for a bit longer. No more picnic lunches with her.

"Good idea. Thanks."

Brock strolled down the buffet, naming off its contents. "I'll text you our orders. You sure you don't mind?"

"Not at all. Any last minute tasks need done at the house?"

"Not a thing. I think Landry has slept better the last few nights than she has in months. You'll never know how much I appreciate you. Bring your lunch and visit with us."

"Glad to be here. I'll have our food over in two shakes of a goat's tail." He went to the kitchen, asked for to-go boxes.

"Better send four." Janice, Chase's mom handed him the Styrofoam containers.

"Why so many?"

"It'll take two for Chase's order, trust me. And one's for salad. Landry always likes salad."

"What kind of dressing?"

"Ranch."

"How much?"

The kitchen door opened and his mom stepped in, gave him a warm smile. "Just checking on the lunch crowd to see when I can start cleaning the dining room."

"Becca, could you help Brock with portions?" Janice grabbed the salad box back from him, handed it to his mom. "He's taking plates over to Chase and Landry."

"Sure." Mom's eyes lit up as if this task was the highlight of her day.

"But remember, she's eating for two."

A few weeks ago, he'd have been livid over this turn of events. "Thanks, Janice." He strolled to the door, held it open for Mom, then followed her into the dining room. There were a few stray guests, but it was mostly empty.

"How about you hold the boxes and I fill them up? Just tell me what she wants."

"Sounds like a plan." He dug his phone from his pocket, read off the text from Chase.

"I was thinking maybe you could join Ron and I for supper tonight." She put lettuce, tomatoes and cucumbers in the box. "Just the three of us this time."

Could he have another nice evening with his mom, without Scarlet and Ruby there as buffers? Or would it get awkward? Her preacher husband was a fine man. Loved the Lord. Spent years working at a dude ranch. They had a lot in common.

And Ron knew the truth now, so he wouldn't have to worry about watching his every word.

Maybe Devree could go with him this time. No. He couldn't get any more attached to her than he already was. His heart couldn't take her nearness, anyway.

"That sounds nice."

The dressing spoon Mom held stopped drizzling. Her hand trembled slightly. "Thank you."

A large lump lodged in his throat. He swallowed. "You're welcome."

Mom set the container filled with salad aside and went to work on the meat and veggies. With a second box finished for Landry, she handed it to him, patted his cheek. "See you tonight." Her eyes closed, voice quivered. "I never thought I'd say that."

"I'll be there." He squeezed her hand.

"Oh, Devree—" Mom looked past him, cleared her throat "—can you help Brock deliver lunch?"

"Sure."

"Thanks." Mom squeezed her arm, hurried to the kitchen.

Devree's questioning gaze met his. "Is she okay?"

"She's emotional. Since the moment I showed up, she's wanted me to come to their house for supper with her and Ron. I finally agreed."

"Want me to go with you?"

Yes. No. Maybe. "I thought about asking you. But sooner or later, we're gonna have to communicate without a referee. Eighteen years doesn't just magically melt away." He picked up four containers. "Ready to go?"

"When did we start delivering lunch?"

"They're for Chase and Landry."

"So this is why they didn't want me to bring anything over for them."

"You checked too?"

"I did. Landry said they were taken care of, but to bring my lunch over and eat with them."

"Chase invited me. Guess we'll be sharing a meal together again." *Great.*

But healing his relationship with his mother, getting to know her, Ron, Scarlet and his niece was worth sticking around for.

He'd just have to grow a tough hide around his heart. At least where Devree was concerned. And as soon as her niece or nephew was born, she'd be out of the picture, anyway. Why did his heart always give a painful tilt at that knowledge?

Chapter Fifteen

Why did she keep getting stuck with Brock? As if the entire dude ranch was conspiring to constantly shove them together.

She stepped up on the new house porch and pressed the bell while holding four food containers. Brock held the other four.

The door swung open and Chase grabbed her load. "Thanks, guys. She's in her fancy living room."

"I heard that," Landry called.

Devree's shoulder brushed Brock's arm. Gooseflesh swept over her, as she hurried through the foyer to the living room. The smile on her sister's face was worth all the hard work.

"It's just feminine." She scanned the floral fabrics, the shabby chic painted furniture and decor in shades of pale green and aqua, with splashes of lilac.

"I think I lost my man card when I walked in." Brock looked around as if really seeing it for the first time. "Can we even eat in here?"

"Oh, shush. Of course not." Landry sat up. "We're going to my new kitchen."

"I'll carry you." Chase started to pick her up.

"If you don't let me walk, I'm going to lose the ability to. And the doctor said I can get up to eat and shower." She stood, waddled toward the kitchen.

Devree grinned. It was sweet and odd to see her normally slender sister so cumbersome.

Landry and Chase settled at the table as Devree and Brock doled out the containers.

"So you like the house?" Devree looked around at the white cabinets, lace curtains and chicken wire accents.

"I love it. You did such a great job. It's just the way I'd have done it."

"Well, you basically coached me through it. I was your hands and feet."

"Ooh." Landry patted her stomach. "Speaking of hands and feet. This little one is really active today."

"Maybe Sprint is hungry." Devree clasped her sister's hand. "Say a prayer, Chase."

"Would you do the honors?" Chase turned to Brock.

He bowed his head and they followed suit. "Dear Lord, thank you for keeping Landry and the baby healthy. Please continue to keep your hedge of protection around them. The Donovans are such a blessing to so many, along with this ranch. Keep everyone here safe and in your will. Thank you for this food and the new friends I've made here. Thank you for repairing my family and helping me decide to make Bandera my home. Amen."

"You're staying?" Landry smiled.

"You still need to hire a new handyman. If that doesn't happen, I'll wait until after the baby comes."

"But I thought you liked it here. You seem so at home and Becca said y'all talked. If you're staying in Bandera, why do we need a new handyman?"

"The ranch will always be close to my heart. But I don't belong here anymore."

"Then where do you belong?" Chase asked.

"In Bandera. Just not in your bunkhouse doing odds and ends. I'm thinking of going back to building cabins. But I won't leave you high and dry."

"I'll admit your talents have been badly underused during your stay." Chase gave him a sheepish grin.

"Thanks to the publicity for Devree's contest, we've gotten several new reservations." Landry dug into her meatloaf. "Maybe eventually, we'll need more cabins built, and we know just the guy to call."

"I hope so."

"Devree's gotten several jobs from the contest too. In Dallas?" A hint of sadness tinged Landry's tone.

"Yes. But not until after the baby is born. And you know I'll be around to visit."

"I just wish you weren't so intent on leaving. Chase and I hoped you'd end up staying too."

"You know my life is in Dallas." Her gaze clashed with Brock's.

Small talk resumed, but Devree kept quiet through the remainder of the meal.

"I better get my princess back to her throne." Chase scooped Landry up.

"I'd love to walk."

"You already did. Only one-way walking, if at all." Chase carried Landry into the living room as Devree and Brock trailed him. As he settled her on the couch, a knock sounded at the door.

"Want me to get that?" Brock offered.

"Please." Chase sat next to Landry with her feet in his lap.

Brock stepped into the foyer, opened the door. "What are you doing here?"

With a wall between them, Devree cringed at the bitterness in his tone.

"I need to see the Donovans." A man's voice.

Chase shot to his feet, strode to the foyer. "How dare you come to my home. Get out."

The door shut. Voices outside. Brock must have gone outside with Chase.

"Who was that?" Devree tried not to sound as worried as she was.

"Judson Tuckerman, a land developer." Landry rolled her eyes. "He's been hassling us to sell. Keeps upping his offer. He ought to catch on by now that this ranch is Chase's family heritage. We'll never sell. And besides that, the property is worth a lot more than he's offering."

"Why does he want it?"

"Who knows. Probably for some housing development or a high-end resort."

The front door opened. "And don't come back," Chase snarled, as he slammed it shut once more.

She'd heard him upset, frustrated, worried, but never like this. Tuckerman must really push Chase's buttons.

"Sorry about that." Chase stalked back into the room.

"What's the big deal?" Devree spread her hands, palm up.

"He had my grandfather's friend almost signing his property over to him for a fraction of what it's worth. Thankfully, his son got wind of it and put a stop to the transaction."

That put Chase's anger in perspective.

"Did Brock leave?" Landry asked.

"He's still trying to talk sense into Tuckerman. Apparently, they were partners a few years back. Probably until Brock figured out what he was about."

Brock worked with Tuckerman? Devree's brain whirled.

"I think we could all use some sweet tea." Chase turned toward the back of the house. "Can you help me with that, Devree?"

"Sure." She followed Chase to the kitchen. Why would Brock work with a land developer who tried to swindle owners into underselling to him? Why would he come to work here as a handyman when he used to build upscale cabins?

Chase grabbed the phone.

"Who are you calling?"

"The sheriff. Get the sweet tea for my cover, will you?"

She filled the glasses while he made the call. As soon as he hung up, he grabbed two teas and started back to the living room.

"Hold up," she whispered. "Brock used to work with the Tuckerman guy."

"Yeah. So?"

"I overheard a phone call a while back. It was someone he'd worked with before and it sounded like they'd ended up on bad terms. After he hung up, he said he had an opportunity for him to get back into building cabins at an upscale resort in a few months."

"That's great. We both know we're wasting his talents here."

"But what if it was Tuckerman? What if he's the one that paid the old handyman to leave? And put Brock up to taking over where Lee Jackson left off? Maybe Brock is scoping out the ranch, trying to figure out a way to get you to sell?"

"No, he's not like that." Chase leaned on the counter.

"Do we really know what he's like? You knew him when you were both kids. He's had a rough life since then."

"He has?"

"Just think about it. He came to work here, way over-qualified. Why?"

Chase looked past her, out the window. "All his memories of his dad are here."

"Or he's still working with Tuckerman and he thinks he has pull with you. Maybe they need this property for their high end resort."

"Come on, Devree, can't you just trust?"

"I've learned there are very few men who can be trusted."

"Well, trust me." Chase held her gaze. "Brock is one of them." He headed back to the living room.

She started to follow, but her cell phone started up and she slid it from her pocket, planning to turn it off. Until she saw the name on the screen. Brighton Electronics.

Had pulling off the perfect dude ranch wedding paid off for her? "Devree Malone speaking."

"Devree. It's Phillip Brighton. How's that daughter and new son-in-law of mine?"

"Week two of living their happily-ever-after, sir. I saw them in the dining room last night, still blissful."

"Good. I've been thinking and I've come to the conclusion that Chasing Eden Dude Ranch is the perfect place for Brighton Electronics' annual company retreat. And you're just the gal to put it all together for me."

"I'd love to work with you again, Mr. Brighton." She tried to keep the exhilaration from her voice, to remain businesslike.

"Can you meet with me tomorrow in Dallas to discuss what I have in mind?"

Tomorrow? Landry had been in the hospital only last week. "Let me check my schedule and see if I can move some things around."

"You do that and call me back."

"You'll hear from me tonight, sir. Thank you."

The line went dead and she pressed her phone to her mouth. How could she leave her sister? They'd always been close and if anything bad happened, she wanted to be here. But Mr. Brighton wasn't known for his patience. If she left him hanging, he might just find another event planner.

By the time she got back to the living room, Chase was back in his usual spot at Landry's feet.

"Devree, you okay?" Her sister's brows scrunched together.

She set the tea glasses on the coffee table, relayed the conversation with Mr. Brighton.

"That's awesome. But why don't you look happy?"

"I can't go to Dallas tomorrow."

"Why not?"

"I can't leave you alone. You were in the hospital last week."

"Look around, I'm not alone with Mr. Hovercraft here."

Chase frowned at the description but didn't argue.

"But I want to stay until Sprint is born."

"Does Mr. Brighton want you to go back to Dallas for good?"

"No. Just to meet with him. An hour. Maybe two, tops." Long enough for Sprint to be born. Or complications to arise.

"I'm fine. You can leave me for a day."

"Mr. Hovercraft is firmly on Landry duty." Chase patted her leg. "I told the staff not to schedule me for anything around here. Go to Dallas if you need to."

"But what if you go into labor?" *Or something goes wrong?*

"I'll call you if I feel the slightest twinge. Dallas is only five hours away and I bet if it was an emergency, Mr. Brighton would fly you on his fancy plane."

"I don't know." She'd never forgive herself if anything happened and she wasn't here for Landry.

"You can't let this opportunity pass you by. It's what you've wanted for months. It'll put your name on the event-planning map and I don't want you to let it slip through your fingers on my account. I'd never forgive myself."

"Are you sure?"

"Positive," Chase interrupted. "You've been slaving on our behalf for weeks. You helped get the honeymoon cottage finished in time for our newlyweds. You pulled off the wedding of the year. And you made this place just the home Landry wanted. She's completely stress-free thanks to you. It's time to do something for yourself for a change."

Her insides warmed. She'd never really known if her brother-in-law liked her. Respected her—yes. Put up with her as part of Landry's package—yes. But she'd always suspected he rolled his eyes over her dirt, insects, reptiles and rodents issues.

"I'll be back tomorrow night."

"You most certainly will not." Landry tsk-tsked. "You can't drive five hours, have a two-hour meeting, then drive five hours back home. You're staying in your apartment tomorrow night. I'll see you Thursday evening."

"I believe that's an order from the honorable Lady Landry." Chase bowed his head.

"I'll be fine. Go make your dream come true. And when you come back, I want to hear all about it."

"Okay. I'll do it. But I mean it, the slightest twinge and you call me. I won't miss Sprint's entrance into the world."

"Promise."

And despite her worries over her sister, an excitement started to build. Dallas. Her apartment. The hustle and bustle of her normal life. The chance to taste it again and build her business.

Lord, keep Landry and the baby safe.

And then it hit her: she'd be leaving Brock behind too. A good thing. Especially if he was in cahoots with this Tuckerman creep. But if Brock stayed, could she leave, knowing he might be conspiring against her sister? Or would she be forced to stay and keep an eye on him? Especially if Chase was wrong about his childhood friend's loyalty.

"Stay away from them, Tuckerman." Brock's jaw clenched. "Chase meant what he said. He's probably called the sheriff by now."

"It's a free country."

"You can't just wander about on private property, especially if the owner wants you to leave and has a *no solicitation* sign up." He jabbed his finger toward the warning in the drive.

"What are you doing working as a handyman here, McBride? With your talent, this is beneath you."

"It's a good place to avoid unscrupulous men like you. I sleep much better at night, knowing I haven't helped swindle any land from befuddled owners."

"You can't tell me you're content with this."

Not entirely, but that was none of Tuckerman's concern. "It was good enough for my dad. It's good enough for me."

"You're happy wrangling goats, cattle and roosters? Not to mention skunks."

Now, it all made sense. "You paid Lee Jackson off to cause trouble around here. Didn't you? To convince the Donovans to throw up their hands and sell to you."

"Lee who? What are you talking about?"

"How else could you know about the hijinks around here?" Heat crawled up his neck.

"I was at that restaurant in town the other day, heard one of your ranch hands talking about it all."

"Uh-huh. If I find out Jackson's on your payroll, you'll be in jail so fast your head will spin."

"I don't know any Jackson. You're barking up the wrong fence post. And you've got no proof."

"If you're involved, I'll find proof, if it's the last thing I do."

A police car pulled into the drive, parked behind Chase's truck and the sheriff got out. "Mr. Tuckerman, how many times do I have to tell you to stay off Mr. Donovan's property unless you're invited?"

"I'm leaving." Tuckerman put his hands up in surrender, hurried to his car, leaving Brock alone with the sheriff.

Should he mention Lee Jackson and his possible connection with Tuckerman? Or just fill Chase in? Knowing Chase, he'd probably want to handle it himself.

"Thanks for coming out." He shook the sheriff's hand.

"Just let me know if he comes back." The sheriff asked Brock a few questions, took some notes, asked him to have Chase call him. He got back into his cruiser, backed out with a wave.

Brock punched Chase's number up. It rang twice.

"Did you get rid of him?"

"The sheriff did. Can you come out for a minute? I have new information."

"Be right there." Chase hung up. Minutes later, he stepped out. "What's going on?"

Brock filled him in on his conversation with Tuckerman.

"Sounds like I need to pay Lee Jackson a visit. Did you mention any of this to the sheriff?"

"No. I figured that was your call."

"Want to go talk to Jackson with me?"

"I have a better idea. You stay here with your wife and let me handle it."

"This isn't your problem."

"No. But you've got enough to deal with. If I can convince Jackson to talk to the sheriff, you'll probably have to come to the station to give a statement. Let me get things rolling for you."

"Make sure Lee knows if he'll tell the sheriff everything, I won't press charges against him." Chase clasped his hand, pulled him into a back slapping hug. "I owe you. A lot." He let go, headed back inside.

Brock hurried to his truck, made the short drive to Jackson's place.

At the door, Brock knocked, waited. No answer. "It's Brock McBride. I know you're in there, Lee. Your truck's here. And I know Judson Tuckerman paid you to disrupt Chase Donovan's ranch. If I can't talk to you about it, I'll talk to the sheriff."

The door opened and a shame-faced Jackson stepped outside. "It wasn't my idea. He sought me out."

"If you're willing to tell the sheriff everything, Chase won't press charges against you."

Jackson blew out a big breath, looked toward the sky. "You promise?"

"He's a man of his word. But if he hears of you getting in any trouble in the future, he will have a talk with the sheriff."

"I'll do it."

"I'll give you a ride."

Brock trailed Jackson back to the truck. Hopefully, this would end Tuckerman's career.

Dressed in her pajamas, Devree threw herself back onto her bed. Home. She dialed Landry.

"How's it going in the Big D?"

"Busy and noisy and wonderful."

"To each his own. Or *her* own, rather."

"You feeling okay?"

"Other than boredom, I'm fine."

"Is Chase with you?"

"No. The supper rush is over, so his mom is babysitting me. Him and Brock are acting weird. I think something's going on with Tuckerman and Chase is trying to shield me. Have you talked to Brock?"

"Um, no. It's not like we're friends or anything." And he might be conspiring against them. But she wouldn't dump that on Landry. Learning of Brock's history with Tuckerman put everything in a new light. It made no sense to her for Brock to apply at the dude ranch as a handyman when he was famous in Texas for building high-end cabins.

"So how'd the meeting go?"

"I aced it. Mr. Brighton hired me to plan his company retreat, and he wants to have it at the dude ranch. We're supposed to get back to him on dates once I get home."

"That's wonderful. If you keep us booked like this, we'll have to hire you as our full-time event planner." Suddenly, Landry gasped.

"What? Is Sprint okay?"

"We're fine. I just realized you called the dude ranch *home*."

"No, I didn't."

"You most certainly did." Landry repeated her words back to her.

"A mere slip of the tongue. Anyway, I'll plan anything you like as long as I can do it from here." She plumped her pillow.

"You still love it there?"

"As much as you loved Aubrey when we were kids. As

much as you love Bandera now. Dallas is where I belong. Here, everything's so filled with purpose and in a rush."

"And that's a good thing?"

"For me, it is. It energizes me. Give baby Sprint a hug for me and I'll see you tomorrow afternoon."

"Drive careful." The call ended.

She snuggled into her pillows, her sheets, turned off the lamp. A siren sounded, grew louder as it neared, then faded away. The buzz and rumble of constant traffic. No crickets. No frogs. She turned on her side, put a pillow over her exposed ear.

Another siren, someone yelling in the street. A boom box with thumping bass from down the hall. She put another pillow over her head, clamped them both to her ear.

In Bandera, when she'd first arrived, she couldn't fall asleep because it was so quiet. But once she'd gotten used to the silence, the peaceful night sounds had lulled her to sleep. There was nothing peaceful about her apartment.

Loneliness swept over her. No one in Dallas loved her. They only wanted her to plan their events.

In the last three weeks, she'd gotten used to having her sister near. And even bonded with her brother-in-law. When Landry had the baby, Devree would miss out on his or her life.

Could it be possible that Dallas wasn't home anymore?

Chapter Sixteen

Piles of planking surrounded Brock as he methodically covered the floor in honeymoon cottage C. Devree had been gone all day yesterday—and she'd left without saying goodbye. But she was supposed to return this afternoon. She might even be here by now. Why was that the thing most prevalent on his mind?

The door opened and she strutted inside. Didn't even spare him a glance. Went straight to the pile of curtains Rustick's had sent over.

"Well, hello to you too. Did you have a nice trip?"

"Yes." Monotone.

"Did you get the job?"

"Yes."

He was sick of the strain between them. So, they'd end up going their separate ways, but it would be nice if the remainder of their ranch days could be stress free.

"You're not gonna make this easy, are you? Can't we get rid of this tension? We still have to work together for a while longer."

She ripped the cellophane package open, jerked out the curtains.

"Are you mad about something?"

She dropped the curtains, turned on him. "Are you in cahoots with Tuckerman?"

"What? No. Of course not."

"It doesn't make much sense for you to go from designing and building luxury cabins to dude ranch handyman."

"Just what are you suggesting?" He pushed to his feet.

"That maybe you're on your former partner's payroll, the way Lee Jackson was. Maybe you've been behind the mishaps around here lately."

"First of all, I was once in a partnership with Judson Tuckerman." Heat moved up his neck. How could she accuse him of being so devious? "But when I realized he was dishonest, I put an end to our affiliation. And second of all, why would I cause mishaps for myself to fix?"

"So you and Tuckerman can get your hands on the dude ranch property no matter the cost."

"You really believe I'd pull something like that?"

"If I find out you've done anything to hurt my sister, you'll regret it. And I think it's best if we work in different areas from now on. I'll do the decor in cottage D while you finish here, then come back and finish up here once you move on." She stalked out, slammed the door behind her.

His stomach sank—he couldn't believe that she'd think him capable of such betrayal. He had to get out of here. Away from the Tuckerman ordeal and now this new source of friction with Devree. He could live somewhere else and still build a relationship with his mother. If only he could cut and run. Leave town, start over somewhere else. Immerse himself in building upscale cabins again.

But he couldn't. He couldn't leave Chase in the lurch. Couldn't let him down. He had to stay—at least until the baby was born.

* * *

The afternoon echoed with bird chatter and song as Devree strode from her car to her sister's porch. Landry swung in the hammock, raised her hand in a wave.

"Did you sleep there?"

"No. But I probably will soon." Landry patted the netting beside her.

"I'll sit in the swing. If I lay down, I might go back to sleep with all this peacefulness." Devree sat in the middle of the porch swing, pushed off with her pointy-toed heel.

"You got the job. I would've thought you'd slept like a baby in your apartment the other night."

"For the first time since I initially moved to Dallas, I heard all the traffic, the sirens, the arguments."

"I knew it. This place has grown on you." Landry wiggled and turned until she faced Devree. "Chase finally filled me in on what's been going on. I can't believe you didn't tell me about all the mice, live traps and cut fences."

"He's the one who said not to tell you. We were trying to keep your stress level at zero. Why did he cave?"

Landry shrugged. "I guess it'll be in the paper since there's been an arrest."

Devree's heart sank. Had Brock been arrested? She hadn't wanted to be right about him. If she was, it would kill Becca.

"I can't believe Tuckerman was behind it all. If Brock hadn't been here and figured it all out, we'd still be in chaos and losing guests."

"Brock figured it out?"

"He convinced Lee Jackson to turn Judson Tuckerman in."

Relief relaxed her tense shoulders. "So Brock wasn't involved."

"Of course not. He and Tuckerman parted ways years ago because Brock realized he was corrupt."

He was innocent. And Devree hadn't believed him. Firmly driving a wedge between them. Even if she decided not to return to Dallas, to stay near her sister and baby Sprint, there was definitely no hope for them now.

A black car pulled in the drive and parked. Resa popped out, hurried to join them as Devree scooted over on the swing.

"Cool hammock." The swing jerked as Resa sat down.

"Chase got it for me for Mother's Day." Landry patted her stomach. "How are you, my long lost friend?"

"I'm absolutely blissful. But I'm a terrible friend."

"Stop. You're busy. With the store, your designing, planning a wedding. You don't have time to babysit me and baby Sprint."

"Sprint?" Resa's eyebrow rose.

Landry laughed, shot Devree a chagrined glare. "You've got me calling him or her that now."

"Chase is the father, so Sprint is the baby." Devree clarified.

"Cute." Resa dug her phone out of her bag. "So I'm dying to marry that man of mine. And I love all the choices you sent me. I found the flowers, colors and decorations I'm going for."

"Let's see what you've got." So much for getting away from weddings. But she couldn't let her friend down. No matter how bad she wanted to.

They compared notes and pictures.

"Can you make it happen?" Resa scrolled through more pictures.

"Of course. But why the great room instead of the chapel?" Devree looked up from the phone.

"My parents were married in the great room. I want to follow their tradition."

"I can't wait." Landry readjusted her weight in the hammock.

"Me neither." Resa clapped her hands. "I was worried. I can't believe you had an opening in June. I assumed it would be your busiest."

"Devree's moving away from weddings into events."

"You can't do that. You're the best wedding planner in Texas."

"Thanks. But I haven't been inspired by my work for a while."

"Some guy broke her heart." Landry's tone echoed certainty.

"Why would you say that?"

"Because I can tell when my sister is hurting. I've been waiting for you to tell me about it."

Landry was right of course. Devree took in a big breath, then filled them in on Randall. How embarrassed she'd been.

"Oh, Devree, I'm so sorry." Landry blew her a kiss from where she lay. "Why didn't you come to me?"

"You were having a difficult time back then. I thought you had enough to deal with."

"I'm never too heartbroken to hear your heartache. But you can't give up on weddings, or men for that matter, because of one jerk."

"Well, I don't think she's given up on men, at least." Resa chuckled. "I saw some pretty impressive voltage between this one and Brock that day in the store."

Devree's face went hot. "Trust me, there was no voltage. We were only working together—trying to turn the fishing cabin into a honeymoon cottage."

"I thought I detected something there also." Landry

waggled her eyebrows. "Something I think you should stick around for."

The front door opened and Chase stepped out. "Lunch is ready."

Devree wanted to hug his neck for saving her from the inquisition. But truth be known, she missed Brock. And it had only been yesterday that they'd decided to work apart.

She'd never been so happy to be mistaken about someone. Now, she had an apology to make. Would he accept it?

She'd pegged Brock completely wrong. She should have known the man determined to smooth the hurt between his mom and stepfather wasn't a man who'd conspire with Tuckerman to attain Landry and Chase's ranch. If she admitted her error, would he forgive her for making the accusation?

Brock stepped out on the back porch of honeymoon cottage E to cut a half inch off the flooring plank. With four cottages complete, Chase had told him to start taking Saturdays off. But that would give him too much time to think.

He looked up when he heard footfalls coming up fast.

Devree darting toward him. Face panic-stricken. Something was wrong.

He rushed to meet her. "What's wrong?"

"Landry's in labor." She held up her keys. "I can't find my key fob and I'm shaking so much I can't get my car unlocked with my spare."

"Give them to me." He grabbed the keys. "You're a mess. Let me drive you."

She nodded, ran to the passenger side as he unlocked the door, flipped the button to let her in.

"They have to be okay. Both of them." She fastened her seat belt.

"Her due date is next week, so everything should be fine."

"This is week thirty-nine. Her stillbirth came at thirty-five weeks. The baby's lungs weren't developed enough." She took a deep breath. "And Landry's had similar complications with this baby."

He grasped her hands. "Dear God, put Your hedge of protection around Landry and the baby. Keep them both safe and healthy. Ease Landry and Chase's fears. Give Devree peace. Hold them all in the palm of Your mighty hand. Amen."

"Thank you." Her voice quivered.

"Where are we going?"

"Fredericksburg. Chase took her for a checkup this morning and the doctor didn't like the baby's oxygen level, so he induced. He said it shouldn't be long now." She sucked in a deep breath, as if ready to do battle. "Landry told me Tuckerman alone was behind all the problems at the dude ranch."

The abrupt subject change caught him off guard. "And you believed her but not me when I told you the same thing?"

"It's hard not to believe since you convinced Lee Jackson to turn him in. But I overheard the conversation you had with a former coworker and assumed…"

"Wallace Montgomery. He's an architect."

"I'm sorry I accused you of still working with him."

"Apology accepted." But the words came out icy.

With her on the edge of her seat, Brock turned the almost one-hour drive into forty minutes, tension propelling him. At the hospital, he let her out at the front door, went to park, then made the trek across the lot, and stepped inside the cool building.

A nurse sat at the desk just inside.

"Landry Donovan?" His nerves were about to jump through his skin.

She pointed to the elevators, gave him the floor.

"Thanks." He strode over, pushed the button. The elevator seemed to move in slow motion.

When it finally opened, he saw Devree sitting in the waiting room, her face in her hands, with Chase's mom patting her arm, his dad pacing.

Bad news? Please, no. "Devree? You okay?"

Her hands dropped away. "Just worried."

"What did they say?"

"That she's progressing nicely and the baby's vitals are strong. I'm sure everything will be fine." Devree's smile quivered. "Chase is in with her."

"What about your folks? Are they coming?"

"Get this." Her chuckle came out high-pitched. "Resa's dad owns a small jet. He sent it to get them."

"That comes in handy."

"They should be here any minute."

As if on cue, the couple he'd seen at church with her hurried toward the waiting room. The man's face was florid, clashing with his red hair. The woman's curly graying brown hair was wild. Her blue eyes—so much like Devree's in color, shape—were filled with worry.

"How is she?" Devree's mom asked.

Devree stood, hugged her mom, shared the latest news.

"No complications?" Her dad waited his turn, then embraced his daughter.

"So far, so good." Elliot shook hands with her dad. "This is Brock McBride, a friend of Chase's. Meet Landry and Devree's parents, Tina and Owen."

They exchanged greetings though obviously distracted. Was it his imagination or did her dad's gaze linger on him a bit long? Had she said something about him to them?

The doctor stepped in the doorway. "Donovan family?"

"Yes," several voices answered in unison.

The doctor smiled. "We have a healthy girl."

"Thank you, God." Devree whispered as relieved and excited words from others blended together.

"What about Landry?" Owen asked.

"She's fine. The baby is seven pounds, six ounces. All her organs are fully formed. You can come back and see her if you like."

All the new grandparents, along with Devree hurried after the doctor.

Brock leaned back in his chair, let the stress ebb away.

"Are they okay?" He opened his eyes to find Resa standing there with a cowboy.

"They're both fine. It's a girl. Their families just went back to see them."

"Oh, what a relief. Her parents got here in time." Resa sank into a chair across from him.

"Thanks to you, I hear."

"Just glad I could help. This is my fiancé, Colson Kincaid. Colson, this is Brock McBride, a friend of Chase's and the dude ranch handyman."

The two men exchanged pleasantries as Colson took his seat beside his bride-to-be.

More people showed up, crowded the waiting room. Some employees along with a few faces he recognized from church, including Mom and Ron.

"Wow, where did y'all come from?" Devree stopped in the doorway.

"Everybody okay back there?" Jed Whitlow asked.

"Just fine, Jed. Landry wants Resa and Chase wants Brock to come see little Eden. You can come too, Colson. After that, they'll take the baby to the nursery and everyone will be able to see her."

Aww's echoed. They'd named the baby after Chase's deceased sister. A lump formed in Brock's throat.

He followed Resa and Colson, trailing behind Devree down a long hall with rooms on each side. Pink or blue bows donned most of the doors. She stopped and opened one with a pink bow. Inside, Janice held a tiny bundle.

"Stop hogging her." Devree plopped down by Chase's mom. "It's my turn since I'm back."

Janice handed the baby over and Devree pushed the blanket back so everyone could see the tiny face framed by dark hair. She looked good cradling the baby in her arms. Natural and content. Like she'd be a great mom someday.

But not to his children. She'd return to Dallas now. And find some businessman in a three-piece suit to give her the happy ending Brock could never provide for her.

Chapter Seventeen

She could leave. So why didn't she want to? Enchanted with the tiny baby in her arms, Devree couldn't take her eyes off her little niece. She'd barely torn herself away long enough to go to church this morning.

"I may never sit down again." Landry strolled around the living room. "Much less lay down. I may sleep standing up, propped against a wall."

Devree chuckled. "Or like a horse, free-standing. I'm glad you're enjoying your mobility."

"I am." Landry eased down on the arm of the couch beside her. "But little Eden was worth it. I'd do it all again— for her."

"She's a doll baby."

"Not enough to keep you here though." Landry sighed. "When are you leaving?"

"I'll stay a few days." Why? Her niece? Yes. The country life? Yes. Brock? Yes. Though there was no hope for them. Not after the way she'd treated him. "I want to get to know little Sprint here."

Landry giggled. "I hope she likes your nickname for her." Landry's phone rang. She stood and dug it from her pocket. "Hey, Becca, everything okay there?" A pause.

"Really? She's right here. What a small world." Another pause. "Sure, I'll send her over."

"You'll never believe who's here."

"Who?"

"The very first couple you married." Landry's eyes sparkled. "They just happen to be here celebrating their eighth anniversary. They were sharing wedding memories with Becca and mentioned what an awesome planner they had in Dallas. Becca realized it was you and told them you're here. They invited you over for lunch at the ranch house."

"They're still married?" Her heart warmed to the point of almost making her teary. "Wow."

"And apparently, happily. Go on over, they're waiting."

She kissed Eden on the forehead, reluctantly handed her over to Landry. "I'll be back, Sprint. Don't you do anything fun without me."

Landry cradled the baby closely as Devree hurried out to her car.

Minutes later, she parked in the dude ranch lot, dashed inside.

Ava and Tyrone Webber waited for her in the foyer. "Devree, it's so good to see you."

"It's good to see y'all." Especially together. She hugged Ava, then Tyrone. Her throat clogged with emotion.

"You've got time for lunch?"

"I do, if you'll let me buy."

"Absolutely not." Tyrone opened the door to the dining room for them.

"I insist. Y'all are just what I needed."

"Why's that?" Ava sat down at a round table.

"I hate to depress you." Devree settled across from her, relayed her post-wedding statistics. "Seeing y'all still living happily-ever-after is a balm to my insecurities."

"You can't blame yourself. What are you doing here? Planning another of your awesome weddings?"

"I did, a few weeks ago. But mainly, I've been here helping my sister out. She was in the last legs of a high-risk pregnancy. But she had my niece yesterday, and they're both fine."

"Wonderful." Ava scanned her menu. "We have two kids. A boy and a girl."

"Really? How old?"

"Six and four."

Tyrone reached for Ava's hand, squeezed it. "And we have Devree to thank."

"I can't take all the credit. God brought you together, and you were smart enough to propose to this beautiful lady."

"He did. And I was. But you made our dream day come true."

Devree stared unseeingly at her menu, even though she knew it by heart. Maybe if she could find a preacher willing to counsel her prospective couples as part of her planning package—focus on the long-term marriage instead of the wedding alone—that would give couples a firmer foundation to start with. Maybe Ron? Probably not, if she returned to Dallas.

If? She didn't even want to anymore. Somehow, Bandera and life in the country had grown on her. It had everything she wanted to stay for. Her sister. Her niece. Brock. But she'd blown her chance with him. She couldn't possibly stay here and see him on a daily basis after the wedge she'd driven between them.

Brock had promised to meet Mom and Ron for lunch, but when he stepped inside the ranch house foyer, Devree was there.

"Hey." She seemed almost shy.

"Hey yourself. I'm meeting Mom and Ron for lunch."

"I was hoping to talk to Ron. Let me run something by you first." Her cell rang and she dug it from her pocket, looking a bit confused when she glanced at the screen. "Unknown number, but it might be a potential client, so I better take it." She swiped the screen. "Devree Malone, at your service. How may I help you?"

Why was he still standing here, watching her, hanging on her every word? He could wait for Mom and Ron in the dining room. Or in the great room. But his feet stayed rooted in place.

"Let me put you on speaker phone, so I can check my calendar." She pushed the button. "What day?"

"October 21. I know it's short notice, but we want to get married on the anniversary of the day we met." The hopeful bride-to-be sounded apologetic.

Barely past mid-May, with October still months away. How long did these shindigs take to set up? And didn't she hate weddings?

"I'm open for that date. Where are you located and where will the ceremony be held?"

"Dallas for both."

"Could we meet next week?"

"Yes, please."

They settled on a day, place and time. Devree put notes in her phone. "You're on my calendar. I'll see you next week." She ended the call.

"I thought you were trying to get out of weddings."

"I know, isn't it crazy?" Genuine excitement lit her eyes. "The thought of another wedding used to make me cringe. But meeting the Hewitts at the river cleanup helped me remember my parents and Landry and Chase are still living happily-ever-after. And I just now had lunch with the first couple I ever planned a wedding for. They're still blissfully happy and have two kids."

"I'm glad you got a glimpse of the sixty percent." He was happy she'd seen the value in weddings. But it was just another reason for her to return to the city.

"Me too. Anyway, it made me rethink some things. I may stick with weddings, but help my couples focus on the marriage more than the ceremony. Do you think Ron would counsel couples for me?"

"You can ask him. But surely there are preachers in Dallas."

"Yes, but I don't know any of them." She ducked her head. "I sort of stopped going to church when I moved there."

"It sounds like you need to find a church home. I mean—if you're staying in Dallas."

Her gaze caught his, sadness looming in their depths. "I'm not cert—"

"Brock, there you are." Mom rushed to embrace him. Since they'd worked things out, she couldn't seem to hug him enough. Trying to make up for a lot of years, he supposed.

"Are you joining us for lunch, Devree?" Ron's gaze bounced back and forth between them.

"I appreciate the offer, but I already ate. I was going to talk to you about something, but it can wait. Enjoy your lunch."

"Let's go in the great room, lunch will keep." Mom locked arms with Devree.

Brock stayed in the foyer.

"Join us, Brock." Mom waved him on. "Unless, it's something private."

"No. I already told Brock about it." Devree glanced back at him.

Mom and Ron took their seats on the couch with Devree and Brock facing them in matching wingbacks.

She quickly summed up her lunch with former clients and the impression the Hewitts had made on her at the cleanup. "It hit me that the thing most of the long-term couples I know have in common is that they're Christians. Some of my couples who've ended up divorced were also, but the majority weren't."

"I don't know how people do marriage without Jesus." Ron shot Mom a loving glance. "Love is a powerful emotion. But you're still dealing with humans, with different backgrounds, needs and annoying habits, then expecting them to live together peacefully."

And secrets that pop up twelve years in. But apparently, Ron had recovered from Mom's dose of reality.

"Exactly." Devree explained her idea. "You could set up a fee and I'd include it in my services package, so you'd be paid for your time. All couples might not take me up on it, but I figure it's worth a shot."

"I'm honored for you to think of me. But can't you find a preacher in Dallas?"

"Honestly and regretfully, I don't know any." She hung her head. "I am planning to change that. But in the meantime, I was thinking we could do phone consultations."

Or maybe she could bring her couples here. Give him a chance to see her every once in a while. *Stop it.* He needed to put her firmly in his past. And when she was forced to return to Bandera, he needed to avoid her like oak wilt. In the same way the disease squeezed the life out of trees, she smothered his heart.

"Tell you what, I'll do it. Until you find someone in Dallas. And if any of your couples need face-to-face in the meantime, I'll commute."

"Thank you. So much."

"My pleasure."

"I'm sure you'll do a great job." Mom squeezed Ron's hand.

"I've held up your lunch long enough." Devree stood. "I'll call you to set up the specifics on counseling."

"We hate to lose you around here." Mom hugged Devree. "I heard you're leaving soon."

"I'm all packed. I plan to spend the rest of the day cuddling my niece and then I'll leave first thing in the morning."

Brock's heart took a nosedive.

"We've enjoyed having you here." Ron followed up with a bear hug.

"Y'all made me feel at home. Even when I didn't." She chuckled. "It's like a great big family around here."

"I know you'll visit with the new baby and all." Mom patted her arm.

"I will. And I'll be back for Resa's wedding next month. Along with a few other events to be held here."

"You be careful, in case I don't see you in the morning."

"I will. See y'all later." Her gaze landed on him, mouth moved, as if she wanted to say something. But she didn't, just turned and then hurried to the foyer.

"Go after her." Mom gave his shoulder a nudge.

"Why?"

"Because you're crazy about her. And she's crazy about you."

"I think the only crazy one around here is you if you believe that."

Mom rolled her eyes. "Ron, talk sense into him. Tell him what a gift love is and that he shouldn't let it slip away."

"Sorry, I gotta sit this one out." Ron checked his watch. "New guests should arrive any minute and I'm on luggage duty. But she's right, I will say that." He strode toward the foyer.

"Why won't you go after her?"

"She accused me of working with Tuckerman, causing all the mishaps around here, so he and I could get the land from Chase and Landry."

"That's all?" Mom splayed her hands, palms upward. "It wasn't a crazy assumption since you used to be partners with Tuckerman."

"Maybe not. But she loves the city. I love the country. She can't wait to get back to her business in Dallas and I can't stand in the way of her dreams."

"Are you certain about that? I think this place grew on her. She almost sounded like she didn't want to leave."

He couldn't listen anymore. "I've got flooring to lay."

He stalked out, but his mom's words echoed through his head. And in his heart. Did Devree really want to leave? Could he stand by and watch her go?

"Don't you dare cry, Landry Ann Malone Donovan." Devree hugged her sister and niece cradled in her arms. "You'll get me started."

"I can't help it." Landry's voice broke. "It's been wonderful having you here. And we didn't really get to enjoy it with me being stuck in a prone position almost the entire time."

"You know I'll be back to visit."

"No, you won't," Landry pouted. "You'll get busy and have an event every weekend, and we won't see you for months at a time."

"Even if that happens, I have to come back next month for Resa's wedding, in July for the Brighton Electronics retreat, and I'll probably get to plan more events here in the future. It'll be the first venue I mention to couples."

"Just don't get too busy for us."

"I won't." She pulled away, kissed Eden's forehead. "You be a good little girl, Sprint."

Landry laughed as Chase carried Devree's suitcases to the foyer. She opened the door for him. With a final wave to her sister, she hurried out to her car, opened the trunk.

"Thanks for coming, Devree." Chase gave her a warm hug. "I don't know what I'd have done without you around here."

"Glad I could help. Take care of them."

"You know I will." He waved, headed back to the house as she got in her car.

She drove into the thicket that separated their home from the dude ranch, then neared the barn. Movement in the goat pen caught her eye. A tiny goat. It seemed Polly had her baby. She parked, got out.

"What a cutie. Polly, you did such a good job."

"Wanna hold her?"

She jumped, clamped a hand to her heart as Brock stepped out from behind the play station. Was it beating out of her chest because he'd scared her? Or because…he was Brock?

"Sorry. I was making sure she gets along with everybody. I just put them back in the pen. Polly was sick of her stall. Do you want to hold little Molly?"

"Can I?"

"Sure."

"How do I hold her?"

"Just like a dog or cat pretty much." He picked up the kid, handed her to Devree.

As his hands briefly touched hers, tingling swept over her skin. "She's so cute." She snuggled the little body close, trying to ignore the effect Brock had on her.

"You off to Dallas?"

She nodded, not trusting herself to speak as her vision clouded. She blinked several times, swallowed hard. "You know when Chase asked me to come, I dreaded staying here. Even though I love my sister. But now, I don't really want to leave."

"Why? I thought you loved Dallas."

"I thought I did. But when I went there last week, it was so noisy I couldn't sleep. And lonely. I guess this place grew on me. I hate leaving Landry, Eden, even little Molly here." But most of all, she hated leaving him.

"Then don't go."

Her breath stalled. Was he just being nice? Or did he care whether she left or not?

"I mean—you shouldn't leave a place if you don't want to."

"But I can't stay here if you hate me."

"I don't hate you, Devree. Far from it."

"I'm so sorry for misjudging you. You didn't deserve it. You're nothing like Tuckerman. Nothing like Randall." She ducked her head. "I'm hoping you'll give me another chance."

Laying her heart bare here. *Please don't crush it.* "See, I'm thinking about staying in Bandera. Since I decided to continue weddings, if I stay here, Ron could easily counsel my couples. And I can base my business anywhere as long as I'm willing to commute."

"I really like that idea."

"You do?"

"I want you to stay, Devree. Not for Landry or Eden. But for me."

Her gaze met his. "You mean to help with the cottages?"

"No. I want you to stay because somewhere between your screaming hysterics over a mouse and you flipping our canoe, I fell in love with you."

Her insides went to mush. "Really?"

"I tried not to. I thought you were city through and through, that you'd leave me behind. But you're not. Not at all. You're loving, caring and tenderhearted."

"I love you too."

"You love me?"

"You had me back when I realized how fully invested you were in protecting Chase and Landry's ranch. No matter the cost to you."

"Does that mean you'll stay?" He pulled her close, with little Molly nestled between them.

"For as long as you want me to."

"How about forever?" His lips met hers.

It was everything she'd ever dreamed of in a kiss.

"Baaaaa." Polly nuzzled Devree's knee.

She giggled, rested her face against Brock's chest, as he kissed the top of her head.

"I think mama goat wants her kid back." He gently took Molly from her, set her down in the pen. "So what's your answer?"

"For some reason, my head is all fuzzy. What was the question?"

"Will you stay with me forever?" He cradled her face in his calloused hands.

"Definitely." She closed the gap between them.

Epilogue

Six months later...

Brock had been so mysterious. Refusing to let Devree decorate the chapel for their wedding. Instead, Landry had acted as her planner, giving her all the choices she usually gave her brides. She could only imagine what it must look like.

"You can open your eyes now, sweetheart." Daddy patted her hand.

She opened her eyes, expecting to be at the chapel doors. Instead, they stood in front of a curtained wall by the river behind Landry and Resa. "What's going on?"

"You'll soon see. Brock wanted to surprise you."

The music began. Landry slipped through the curtain, carrying Eden. Seconds passed before Resa disappeared through the drapery. The music swelled and transitioned into the traditional "Wedding March." The curtains were swept aside to reveal a long white walkway with a gazebo at the end. And Brock grinning at her. Dressed in jeans and a blazer with a white rose on his lapel. No girly-colored vest required.

"We don't have a gazebo," she mumbled.

"He built it for you. Ready to do this?"

Her heart fluttered. "I was ready six months ago."

They walked slowly down the aisle, like she'd shown all her brides. Tulle and twinkle lights draped in the trees over their heads, with satin bows on the back of each white chair. Beautiful. But none of it mattered in comparison to her groom and the future stretching before them.

She'd come here to help her sister and plan a wedding. She hadn't counted on falling in love. But now, she was definitely counting on the cowboy. Forever.

* * * * *

If you loved Brock and Devree's story,
be sure to pick up the rest of the titles in the
TEXAS COWBOYS *series:*

REUNITING WITH THE COWBOY
WINNING OVER THE COWBOY
A TEXAS HOLIDAY REUNION

Available now from Love Inspired!

Find more great reads at www.LoveInspired.com

Dear Reader,

I once considered myself a city girl. When my parents moved me from a suburb of Atlanta to rural Arkansas, I thought my life was over. Until I met a transplanted Texan who made me realize country life wasn't so bad. Thirty-eight years later, I wouldn't want to live anywhere else.

I put a lot of me in Devree. She doesn't like to get dirty, has no appreciation for most farm animals and isn't the out-doorsy type. But the quiet, simple life slowly grows on her.

Polar opposites from two different worlds always fascinate me. Enter Brock with his broken heart thanks to a city girl—he's determined to avoid falling for Devree from the beginning.

But slowly, they see past their initial assumptions about each other and begin to realize they have more in common than they ever would have thought. Until finally their defenses slip away, as God mends their hearts.

This book wraps up my Texas Cowboys series. That always makes me sad as I'll miss living and breathing their stories. I hope you love each couple as much as I do.

Blessings,
Shannon Taylor Vannatter

COMING NEXT MONTH FROM
Love Inspired®

Available April 17, 2018

THE WEDDING QUILT BRIDE
Brides of Lost Creek • by Marta Perry

Widowed single mom Rebecca Mast returns to her Amish community hoping to
open a quilt shop. She accepts carpenter Daniel King's offer of assistance—but
she isn't prepared for the bond he forms with her son. Will getting closer expose
her secret—or reveal the love she has in her heart for her long-ago friend?

THE AMISH WIDOW'S NEW LOVE
by Liz Tolsma

To raise money for her infant son's surgery, young Amish widow Naomi Miller
must work with Elam Yoder—the man she once hoped to wed before he ran
off. Elam's back seeking forgiveness—and a second chance with the woman he
could never forget.

THE RANCHER'S SECRET CHILD
Bluebonnet Springs • by Brenda Minton

Marcus Palermo's simple life gets complicated when he meets the son he never
knew he had—and his beautiful guardian. Lissa Hart thought she'd only stick
around long enough to aid Marcus in becoming a dad—but could her happily-
ever-after lie with the little boy and the rugged rancher?

HER TEXAS COWBOY
by Jill Lynn

Still nursing a broken heart since Rachel Maddox left town—and him—years
earlier, rancher next door Hunter McDermott figures he can at least be cordial
during her brief return. But while they work together on the Independence
Day float, he realizes it's impossible to follow through on his plan because he's
never stopped picturing her as his wife.

HOMETOWN REUNION
by Lisa Carter

Returning home, widowed former Green Beret Jaxon Pruitt is trying to put down
roots and reconnect with his son. Though he took over the kayak shop his
childhood friend Darcy Parks had been saving for, she shows him how to bond
with little Brody—and finds herself wishing to stay with them forever.

AN UNEXPECTED FAMILY
Maple Springs • by Jenna Mindel

Cam Zelinsky never imagined himself as a family man—especially after making
some bad choices in his life. But in seeking redemption, he volunteers to help
single mom Rose Dean save her diner—and soon sees she and her son are
exactly who he needs for a happy future.

**LOOK FOR THESE AND OTHER LOVE INSPIRED BOOKS WHEREVER
BOOKS ARE SOLD, INCLUDING MOST BOOKSTORES, SUPERMARKETS,
DISCOUNT STORES AND DRUGSTORES.**

LICNM0418

Get 2 Free Books,
Plus 2 Free Gifts—
just for trying the Reader Service!

Love Inspired®

YES! Please send me 2 FREE Love Inspired® Romance novels and my 2 FREE mystery gifts (gifts are worth about $10 retail). After receiving them, if I don't wish to receive any more books, I can return the shipping statement marked "cancel." If I don't cancel, I will receive 6 brand-new novels every month and be billed just $5.24 for the regular-print edition or $5.74 each for the larger-print edition in the U.S., or $5.74 each for the regular-print edition or $6.24 each for the larger-print edition in Canada. That's a saving of at least 13% off the cover price. It's quite a bargain! Shipping and handling is just 50¢ per book in the U.S. and 75¢ per book in Canada.* I understand that accepting the 2 free books and gifts places me under no obligation to buy anything. I can always return a shipment and cancel at any time. The free books and gifts are mine to keep no matter what I decide.

Please check one:
- ☐ Love Inspired Romance Regular-Print (105/305 IDN GMWU)
- ☐ Love Inspired Romance Larger-Print (122/322 IDN GMWU)

Name _____ (PLEASE PRINT)

Address _____ Apt. #

City _____ State/Province _____ Zip/Postal Code

Signature (if under 18, a parent or guardian must sign)

Mail to the **Reader Service:**
IN U.S.A.: P.O. Box 1341, Buffalo, NY 14240-8531
IN CANADA: P.O. Box 603, Fort Erie, Ontario L2A 5X3

Want to try two free books from another line?
Call 1-800-873-8635 today or visit www.ReaderService.com.

*Terms and prices subject to change without notice. Prices do not include applicable taxes. Sales tax applicable in N.Y. Canadian residents will be charged applicable taxes. Offer not valid in Quebec. This offer is limited to one order per household. Books received may not be as shown. Not valid for current subscribers to Love Inspired Romance books. All orders subject to approval. Credit or debit balances in a customer's account(s) may be offset by any other outstanding balance owed by or to the customer. Please allow 4 to 6 weeks for delivery. Offer available while quantities last.

Your Privacy—The Reader Service is committed to protecting your privacy. Our Privacy Policy is available online at www.ReaderService.com or upon request from the Reader Service.

We make a portion of our mailing list available to reputable third parties that offer products we believe may interest you. If you prefer that we not exchange your name with third parties, or if you wish to clarify or modify your communication preferences, please visit us at www.ReaderService.com/consumerchoice or write to us at Reader Service Preference Service, P.O. Box 9062, Buffalo, NY 14240-9062. Include your complete name and address.

LI17R3

SPECIAL EXCERPT FROM

Love Inspired®

Widowed single mom Rebecca Mast returns to her Amish community hoping to open a quilt shop. She accepts carpenter Daniel King's offer of assistance—but she isn't prepared for the bond he forms with her son. Will getting closer expose her secret—or reveal the love she has in her heart for her long-ago friend?

Read on for a sneak preview of
THE WEDDING QUILT BRIDE
by *Marta Perry,*
available May 2018 from Love Inspired!

"Do you want to make decisions about the rest of the house today, or just focus on the shop for now?"

"Just the shop today," Rebecca said quickly. "It's more important than getting moved in right away."

"If I know your *mamm* and *daad*, they'd be happy to have you stay with them in the *grossdaadi* house for always, ain't so?"

"That's what they say, but we shouldn't impose on them."

"Impose? Since when is it imposing to have you home again? Your folks have been so happy since they knew you were coming. You're not imposing," Daniel said.

Rebecca stiffened, seeming to put some distance between them. "It's better that I stand on my own feet. I'm not a girl any longer." She looked as if she might want to add that it wasn't his business.

No, it wasn't. And she certain sure wasn't the girl he remembered. Grief alone didn't seem enough to account for the changes in her. Had there been some other problem, something he didn't know about in her time away or in her marriage?

He'd best mind his tongue and keep his thoughts on business, he told himself. He was the last person to know anything about marriage, and that was the way he wanted it. Or if not wanted, he corrected honestly, at least the way it had to be.

"I guess we should get busy measuring for all these things, so I'll know what I'm buying when I go to the mill." Pulling out his steel measure, he focused on the boy. "Mind helping me by holding one end of this, Lige?"

The boy hesitated for a moment, studying him as if looking at the question from all angles. Then he nodded, taking a few steps toward Daniel, who couldn't help feeling a little spurt of triumph.

Daniel held out an end of the tape. "If you'll hold this end right here on the corner, I'll measure the whole wall. Then we can see how many racks we'll be able to put up."

Daniel measured, checking a second time before writing the figures down in his notebook. His gaze slid toward Lige again. It wondered him how the boy came to be so quiet and solemn. He certain sure wasn't like his *mammi* had been when she was young. Could be he was still having trouble adjusting to his *daadi*'s dying, he supposed.

Rebecca was home, but he sensed she had brought some troubles with her. As for him…well, he didn't have answers. He just had a lot of questions.

Don't miss
THE WEDDING QUILT BRIDE by Marta Perry,
available May 2018 wherever
Love Inspired® books and ebooks are sold.

www.LoveInspired.com